KISS ME WITH YOUR DOE EYES

MONICA SAHU

INDIA · SINGAPORE · MALAYSIA

KISS ME WITH YOUR DOE EYES

MONICA SAHU

ISBN 979-8-89186-798-7

CONTENTS

AUTHOR'S NOTE

This fictional story is not based on any person, any event or any place in real life. Coincidental similarities, if any, are certainly unintentional.

Readers are advised to treat this story as a form of entertainment and not a self help book on how to deal with similar situations in real life.

Some parts of this story may trigger sensitive audiences who have experienced bullying and abusive environments.

This book is not suitable for kids and younger teens.

The scanning, uploading and distribution of this book via the Internet as well as the replication, printing and sale via any vendor, without the permission of the publisher and author, is illegal and punishable by law.

Please purchase only authorized print and electronic editions and do not engage in or encourage piracy of copyright materials.

Your support of author's rights is highly appreciated.

READING INSTRUCTIONS

All chapters are in chronological order.

Chapters 1 to 6 and 9 are from the POV of the protagonist.

Chapter 7 and 8 are from different points of view and narrator details are mentioned before the beginning of said chapters.

Diary Entry pages are from the POV of a male character.

They contain sensitive content like mention of bullying.

EPILOGUE is from the POV of said male character.

This book is best enjoyed after reading it's prequels.

- A FAMILY OF STRANGERS
- THE STRANGE REALITY

Happy Reading!

CHAPTER 1

A COZY CAFE AROUND THE CORNER

Adulthood is complicated. Because, if you think rationally, how can a certain age determine the extent of our social independence?

My brother and I might have never moved out of our family home, unless we were kicked out, during our thrilling and terrifying twenties. It's a family tradition. Everyone must learn to survive on their own, if they wish to be a part of the family legacy.

If it was up to us, we would have never ventured out on our own. We might have spent a lifetime in the confines of the walls erected by our ancestors. Because, living on your own is not that fun.

You need a source of income, a home where you feel safe, and, maybe, a person who knows exactly how to comfort you. To make things easier, you can opt for a stable job with a set work schedule and enough time for socializing. And, while a job has it's own set of stress-inducing responsibilities, it comes with perks like a steady paycheck and a definitive day off, every single week.

But, when you wish to start your own business, you can say goodbye to date nights, weekend getaways and breakfast-in-bed. Instead of waking up next to your partner or a plate full of pancakes, you might wake up next to a heap of unpaid bills and a half-eaten slice of pizza that sticks to your face. It's aromatic sauce might even smear on your cheeks a lot better than your expensive moisturizer.

In addition to sacrificing your chances of having a relationship, you will also need to accurately time your professional arrival. Too soon and your vivid entrepreneurial ideas may not be appreciated. Too slow and your business might drown in competition.

When I moved out of our family home and started living on my own, knocking the right doors and shaking the right hands became imperative. And that's how I met my favorite person in this city.

It was raining, on that unusual summer day, when I bumped into my realtor. She was setting up a plate of chocolate chip cookies and turning on the coffee machine as I entered the beautiful apartment. The walls were warm and welcoming. A giant window was lighting up the place with a calming, golden glow. And the intricately designed rug was so beautiful, until I tripped on it.

While I was stumbling and struggling to find my footing, I could see her rushing towards me. A half-full box of cookies was immediately sacrificed and the saccharine snacks were dramatically flying across the room. One had landed on the couch and a few were on the kitchen counter. But, before I could even understand that I was not going to break my fall on my own, she had gently caught me in her arms.

The moment must have looked like a poster for any classic romantic comedy. And it even came with a funny twist. The cookie crumbs, that made it's way to me, had quickly stuck to my slightly damp satin dress and started staining the pearl-white fabric. Imagine having to explain chocolate stains to your highly imaginative and slightly mischievous dry-cleaners.

"Are you okay?" she had asked me.

It was a simple question and she sounded genuinely concerned about me. But simplicity had never been a part of my life. So, I had cried for what felt like an eternity.

She never asked me to stop or pull myself together. Instead, she held my hand as I poured my heart out. My words slurred on my trembling tongue and tear stained lips. But, she kept nodding and kept listening.

No one had ever asked me if I was okay. In fact, I had never asked myself if I was okay. But, after talking to her about everything that I had been thought, and after seeing how she did not judge me, I knew that I needed her in my life, just as much as I needed a home.

At that time, I had no idea how that one interaction was about to change my life. And whenever I think about that moment, I wonder how my life would have been like, had I never met her.

Life keeps reminding us that, the concept of free will, is not as simple as it seems. Every step we take and every hand we shake, can lead us to a completely new future. In fact, the trajectory of our lives can often be dictated by complex emotions.

So, can we choose to live any differently, if we know what the future holds? Can we make better choices, cut bitter ties or forge more beneficial bonds, if we know exactly how those decisions will effect our future?

These are some of the questions that I ask myself, on restless night, while thinking of all my major life choices, until I am too tired to keep my eyes open. And, each morning, I wake up with a different mood.

Today's mood is joyful, for now.

A bright day has arrived, birds are chirping at a distance, and the sky is clearer, after having rained all night. Even the delicate rays of the early morning sun, are glittering on the walls that surround me.

Something about the day feels safe, warm and fresh. It's just like a cup of freshly brewed coffee or a loaf of freshly baked bread.

Color-coded sticky notes are dancing, happily, next to the fridge magnets that my brother keeps sending me. He calls them his "I miss you" presents. I have one from every country he has visited. And my favorite is the golden one, shaped like an egg, that holds my to-do list in place.

I take a quick peak out of my living room window while sipping my morning cup of coffee. It's such a quite and peaceful day. The streets aren't as noisy as they usually are. Even the cabs are shining under the sun, resting near the curb as they wait for passengers.

What a beautiful day!

When I finally step out of my apartment, I notice a moving truck pulling over, right across the street from my building. It seems like a piano is being delivered. We may finally have a fancy neighbor.

I quickly cross the intersection and continue walking down the street to my favorite place in the city. It's just around the corner from the flower shop and everything smells like a spring day. Fresh, breeze and relaxing!

The air feels especially crisp as I walk past a bunch of flowers being unloaded from a van and being rushed into the shop. I embrace the fragrances with a deep inhale and continue walking, happily. There is even an unusual spring in my stride.

Days like this are rare, precious.

As I inch closer to my destination, I reach the intricately crafted metal gates of the compound. Our cafe is the main attraction of the block. It has been a must-visit foodie destination for a few months now. We seem to be doing everything right, so far. And I absolutely love how close it is to my home.

When I walk into the compound, I notice a table near the entrance, that looks a little out of place. It's no big deal. I know exactly how to bring it back to it's rightful place.

So I walk in and hold the misplaced table by the edge. I've done it before. It's not that heavy. And, as I am pulling it back to it's usual spot, I finally notice it.

IT ALWAYS GETS LOUD
BEFORE IT GETS QUITE

I run my fingertips over the words that are carved into the wooden surface of the table. Each letter is etched in with more rage than the previous one. The last word is barely legible.

Who could have done such a thing?

Was it a disgruntled former employee, a drunk patron or just a random passerby? Or maybe it was that intern who kept drinking more coffee than he sold?

Is this revenge?

It seems too small for a revenge but the words feel too heavy for a prank. The doubts, questions and speculations keep roaring in my head like the sounds of an approaching thunderstorms. It's loud. Too loud.

It would be wise to go inside and check the footage from the security camera. It must have recorded something, right? After all, that's what it's there for.

As I reach into my bag, the metal clasps seem too tight for my sweaty fingertips. And, as I fumble with the keys for the front entrance of the cafe, I notice that the glass doors are already unlocked.

It's so easy to panic but I try to steady my nerves and remind myself that it must be one of our employees. Maybe one of the girls came in before I did. They do that, sometimes. Or maybe it's the baker, opening up early, for the morning rush.

gasp

The morning rush! It's a public holiday. The streets would not be quite for too long. We have to get ready before people start pouring in.

As I rush into the back office to check the security footage, I find my business partner, fiddling with the keyboard. His doe eyes are glued to the screen.

When I set my bag down, it's metal buckle hits the shiny metal surface, making the table ring like a bell.

"Oh! You're here! Come! Check this out!" he says while turning the computer screen towards me.

The timestamp reads quarter past midnight. A man, wearing a black raincoat, has been recorded while scratching words into the wooden table, with what looks like a sharp knife. He seems angry. But why? What did the table do to him? Did it stub his toe?

My coping mechanism is on overdrive.

"This goes on for a while? Should I skip ahead?" my diligent business partner questions with his big, beautiful eyes fixated on my furrowed brows. So I straighten the wrinkles on my forehead and I nod.

Where the timestamp reads half past midnight, the man seems done carving the words with shaky hands. He then kicks the table to watch it topple and roll. But he catches it, right before it hits the glass door, maybe to avoid ringing the safety alarms. He then clumsily picks it up and sets it down, as close to it's original spot as possible.

I might have never seen such a theatrical act of vandalism and I might be a little amused. But my business partner is practically beaming with joy. And I'm not sure if he is more excited about the theatrics or the vandalism itself.

Maybe I need to run another background check on him.

"Send a copy of this video to Sophie and let her handle it, okay?" I instruct him while taking off my coat which always gets stuck, somewhere between my shoulders and my elbows. And it's always a new and increasingly painful position to be stuck in.

Maybe I need a new coat. This one does not fit me anymore. Stress and sweat are never helpful. But, at least, I do not have to worry about my looks around here. It's not like I need to impress a man with my measurements, unless I'm measuring ingredients for the morning specials. And I'm getting too old to care about what others think of me.

And who would I even impress? There is no one around to even peak my interest. Not even my beautiful, brilliant, doe eyed baker and business partner. I do not like him! He is way too young for me. And he gets excited about odd things.

Am I odd enough for him?

"Hahaha! Look! He even yelled at the camera before he left!" my annoyingly beautiful business partner looks ecstatic.

Does he have to be so pretty?

My hair is turning a far more uneven shade of gray than his seemingly flawless skin. Does he put on more make up than I do? Or is it just his natural skin? Seriously, why is he so beautiful?

And why does he find this vandalism so amusing? Does he know something that I don't? Is he involved in this incident, somehow? Does he know the man who did this? Did he put someone up to scare me? Am I being too paranoid or too careless about this beautiful, over qualified man?

gulp

I definitely need to ask Sophie to run another background check on him.

"Who's on duty today?" I ask, while checking the staff register.

"Sarah had to take a few days off because of her ankle. She said she should be back by Monday. Tanya offered to fill in for her."

"Hmmm! But please ask someone else to fill in for Sarah's shift tomorrow, since it's Tanya's day off."

"Already did! It's all sorted out! I've even noted down the changes in the register." he smiles at me with a look of sincerity. Or maybe it's condescension? I don't quite understand him yet. His broad shoulders always get in the way of my better judgement.

I flip the pages and check, only to find his obnoxiously beautiful handwriting next to my aging alphabets. Even my As and Bs are curved like a C. Maybe they are aging, just like I am. Meanwhile, his handwriting looks like a calligraphy tutorial.

Why is he so...so...

sigh

That's it! I'm calling Sophie for a girls-night-in. She can have my stash of wine while listening to me cry over my over-qualified, dashing and slightly suspicious business partner.

• *Diary Entry* •

I'm not sure how THIS is supposed to help me with my anxiety. But, I'm going to give it a try.

My therapist thinks that it can help me remember the little derails about that incident. But, I've never forgotten about that day, not even a little bit.

Writing about it, after such a long time, is only going to hurt like a hot knife running into a stick of butter. So, how can it possible help me heal?

But, I'm trying to trust his professional opinion and hoping that it will bring me some peace of mind. And honestly, I'm not sure why he wants me to share this diary with her, if I ever meet her again.

So, if you are reading this, I hope you can forgive me for what I did in the past. It was never my intention to hurt anyone. But, I always seem to end up in the eye of the storm.

It all started when they saw me! They had barged into the old A/V room, thinking that it would be empty, like it usually was. And I tried to hide behind the janitor's cart in the desolate hallway. But, that dang broom fell and caught their attention.

There was nowhere else to go and the dingy basement was my only option. The old bathrooms near our old A/V room, were being renovated at snail's pace. So, I decided to hide inside the last stall, the one with the demo installations.

The stall smelled like fear and desperation mixed with bleach. No one ever entered that stall unless they were trying to hide.

Some hid their shame, some hid their desires, some hid their fears. I was hiding my disbelief and disgust. But, I did not expect them to follow me, even when I knew what they did in the abandoned parts of our campus.

There were footstep from three, or maybe four people. I could recognize three of them but, I wondered who the fourth person could be. I wondered if it was someone I cared for.

It took me a while to recognize who the fourth person was. And, I'll never forget what I heard next.

CHAPTER 2

THE SECRET TO A LONG FRIENDSHIP

There are two things that are guaranteed, when Sophie comes home. She will always bring a big bucket of cheese flavored popcorn. That part is highly appreciated. The second one, manages to freak me out, every single time.

While it is not something that is unforgivable, it definitely makes me cringe. Why? Because she will touch the one thing in the apartment that she is forbidden to get her cheese coated fingers on.

"Can you, for once, spare my precious vinyls?"

I protest, every time she visits. But she never listens. Instead, she smirks as she pulls her favorite record out of the shelf and hands it to me.

"Here! Play this for me before I get drunk and start making out with your gorgeous neighbor.".

"Didn't you do that, last time? Shouldn't you be moving on to the next step by now?"

"What next step?" she yells but it sounds heartbroken. And I think I know how she feels.

We have had a long week. The holiday rush kept me busy and Sophie was juggling her clients along with the cafe vandal situation. I want to ask her if she found out something about the man. But tonight might not be the best time for that. It can wait.

"There! Let's dance!" I play the track and offer her my hand. And, as always, she rushes towards me and wraps me in her arms.

"DO NOT STAND ON MY *OUCH* FEET!"

I yell, every single time, but she never listens. And what am I supposed to do? Push her away? Like everyone pushes me away? Call her clingy? Like everyone calls me?

No! Never!

"Hmmm! This is nice!" Sophie sighs and rests her chin on my shoulder. It's convenient when two people, any two people, are comforted by touch.

This has become our ritual by now. We dance, we drink wine and we cry over people who hurt us. Sometimes, we even cry over expectations that hurt us. This is exactly why we have been best friends, for such a long time.

Since I moved here, right after a series of bad decisions, I needed a fresh start and an escape from my persistent patterns. But, my family was against it. They thought that it was going to be another one of my impulsive life choices that bite me back when I least expect it.

My family loves me. But they seldom understand me. Their idea of a happy life, is nothing like my own. And, apart from my brother, they seldom forget the mistakes that I make.

So, with each passing day, I needed to get away from everyone who reminded me of all my terrible life choices, so far. And that's exactly why I picked this city, an entire timezone away from my family.

Sophie helped me with everything, from finding the right apartment to starting my own business. She was supposed to be "just a realtor". But I quickly realized that she had way too many tricks up her silken sleeves.

At some point, my business ideas needed someone who understood baking, better than I did. Someone who studied baking, unlike me who studied finance and ditched a position in my brother's business, just to start my own little gluten and caffeine nook. That's what my brother called it, when he visited my first cafe, right after I settled into my new life in this new city.

I miss him.

A cafe was an even bigger undertaking than paying mortgage for an overpriced home. There was only so much that I knew about handling a business in a bustling city with intense competition. And my extravagant business ideas, needed a better location with doorman buildings and disposable income.

That was when my mysteriously generous investor and business partner, just fell into my lap. Someone introduced us at an events and he seemed to love my ideas, enough to want to work with me. It felt like finding everything I was looking for, all in one place, all at the same time.

Ever since I moved into this city, life has just been kind. So kind.

Too kind.

I may sound paranoid but, this sudden, comfortable living, makes me anxious. I wonder if it's just the universe paying me back for all that I've been thought. Or is it just another twist, silently brewing around the corner?

I know that it may sound unfair but, my beautiful, wealthy and brilliant business partner, is turning my hair gray from worrying about his motives. And I'm way too young to have gray hair. My thirties have only just begun.

Today's mood was dominated by bitterness and confusion, until Sophie came home. She can make any day better, just by being there, right by my side. I wonder if that's the reason why I don't feel the need to hang out with my other friends. I have her, all of her.

She is mine!

"Hey, Sophie?"

"Hmmm?"

"Do we know enough about Jay?"

"Why? Is he bothering you? Did he set the oven on fire, again? Do you need a new business partner?" Sophie sounds frantic, just like the quintessential best friend character in any romantic comedy, who will always have your side, even before knowing who you're fighting.

"No! Nothing like that! But..."

"Oh! So is he being weird, after the vandalism? Do you want me to dig in, a little deeper, again?"

She knows me so well! Maybe that's the reason why we have been best friends for so long.

"Well, can we? I mean, is there anything left to find out about him?" I ask while Sophie let's go of me and grabs the wine bottle from the kitchen counter.

"Anything specific you would want me to look into?" she takes a sip after asking. And by sip, I mean a few, breathless gulps. I wonder what's worrying her. Maybe I should ask her that? Or maybe we need to figure it all out, one thing at a time.

"Well, he just seems...too...you know?"

Did I just blush? My cheeks feel warm as I try to think of the right way to phrase my statement.

"Too...what?" she smirks. I wonder why she smirked. Maybe she saw me blushing. That's embarrassing. I hope she does not read too much into it.

So I reply, with deep restraint on my emotions "Too good to be true! You know what I mean?". Because it really might sound like I'm into him. I'm not! I really am not! It's just the wine that's making me feel a little flushed.

Sophie laughs and asks "Babe! Be honest, okay? Does it bother you that a good looking, wealthy, talented, gentle and dedicated man, likes you? I mean I know it acts a bit strange sometimes but...".

"Likes me?" I scoff before she can finish her sentence. Because, it's a preposterous thought to ponder on. Why would he like me? We are just business partners and I can't possibly be his type, not that he is my type. His flawless self seems unreal to me.

"Think about it! He had his own cafe. He could bake, way better than you ever could. And he still let you become a co-owner of his business. Do you think it's because he likes your ideas? And yes, I know, your ideas are amazing. Your creations have become a penthouse breakfast and brunch party must-have! But still! Couldn't he have just hired you, instead of making you an equal partner in his established business?"

"Maybe he saw potential in me, as a business partner." I protest while grabbing the wine bottle from her hand to take a sip. And by sip, I mean, just a sip. Getting drunk has never been useful for me.

But Sophie laughs again and grabs the bottle back from my grasp before responding "Or maybe it's because he sees potential in you, as a person, in whatever way you peak his interests."

Whatever way? I wonder what that means! But I don't ask her any more questions. She has already chugged down half a bottle of wine. A sober Sophie is far more logical than a drunk, dazed and dreamer Sophie. Anything she says, right now, will come from a romantic part of her heart, that flutters from the most absurd and imaginary possibilities.

Maybe I'll ask more when she comes back with some information about the vandal. I seriously hope that it's not my business partner's plan to scare me away and kick me out of our business.

Everyone knows about the value I add to the business. I've definitely helped him grow over the past few months. This is my business, just as much as it is his. We are equal partners. Do I need to remind him of that?

But Sophie is right about one thing. He had enough to make it work on his own. So why did he agree to become equal partners? Why was he so interested in me?

I need to find out a little more about him! And I need to know who that vandal was. Something about that man seemed a little too familiar. Maybe I should check the video again. Because, I feel like I have seen that raincoat before.

"Alright! I'm going to make out with your gorgeous neighbor now!" Sophie announces after she chugs down the rest of

the wine and heads towards the door on wobbly
legs.

I would be worried if I did not know that my next door
neighbor is Sophie's on-again off-again husband.

Yup! Husband!

My best friend has married, divorced, remarried and re-
divorced the same man, over and over again.

Is re-divorced even the right word? Do I want to care about
every little unique word in the dictionary?

So what, if I use some made-up words from time to time?
Aren't all words just made up? Can't we just focus on the
emotions?

More importantly, I don't even know how someone finds
a man like that. A man who put up with someone so
impulsive? I had no idea that men like him even existed in
our generation.

Sophie is a sweetheart but I seriously can't imagine waking
up to her emotional rollercoaster ride, every single day. Her
ex is either a saint for putting up with it or an emotional
masochist for going along with her extreme and impulsive
decisions.

I was taught to be grateful for people who show me love,
especially in a relationship. I was taught to give back more
than I received. And I was always giving more of me with
every passing day. Maybe that's why I never found someone

who treated me like an equal partner. Or maybe it's because of my very own Achilles heel.

Maybe my over-thinking is just as annoying as Sophie's impulsiveness! But no one puts up with my doubts and fears. So, maybe, I'm a little annoyed by how some people get so many second chances. I deserve one too. I think I do.

No! That's not good enough!

I know for a fact that I deserve a second chance.

But why am I even comparing my life with the one friend who is kind to me? The only friend who is just as miserable as I am? Maybe that's why we have been best friends for so long.

GRUNTS

I smack my head with the empty wine bottle. Another tradition, I guess.

Even the empty bottle, rolls away from me, when I try to set it down. And my sleep left the apartment when Sophie left. It all feels empty again.

I wonder if I should just make some breakfast for her. A cake, perhaps? She always craves a red velvet cake after a drunken "mistake" with her ex.

SIGH

When and where will I ever find someone to make a drunken mistake with? And, how can I even trust anyone for something so impulsive? I keep asking questions to myself as I drag myself to the pantry.

My color-coded sticky notes, usually dance, every time a gust of wind comes to greets them. But, when I walk past them, all they do is flutter, like my tired eyelashes. One even decides to fall and slip under the refrigerator. So, I grab a spatula and pull it out before sticking it back, right where it belongs.

"Don't you dare give up on me! We have unfinished business, got it?" I sternly pat the sticky note. Because, who else will remind me that I have a dentist appointment on Monday, if the sticky note decides to fall, again? I'm too old-fashioned to rely on anything other than my colorful stationary.

After making sure that none of the other sticky notes can take an unscheduled flight, I get to the pantry and grab a box of all-purpose flour. It's the last one on the top shelf, the one I kept for emergencies.

"Ugh! There's so much to do! Now I gotta go buy groceries. When will my life get easier? Why can't I have someone who can do all these things for me?"

I'm frustrated and too exhausted to feel any emotions, at least for the night. But, deep down, I keep dreaming of a time when my pantry will be full, even when I forget to buy groceries.

As I'm grabbing the supplies to make Sophie's cake, I hear something from across the main door.

knock knock knock

"Did you forget something?" I asks, because, it has to be Sophie. Who else could possibly come over, at one in the morning? None of my other friends know my home address, and my family lives an entire timezone away.

I set the box down, on a corner of the kitchen counter, and drag myself to open the door, just wide enough to take a peak. And I see a pair of big, beautiful, doe eyes, staring back at me.

"What the heck are you doing here, right now?" I ask Jay, who looks even more beautiful in the darkness of night. The dim corridor lights, that makes me look like a side character from a horror movie, is making him look like the lead from classic romantic movies.

He even smiles like the quintessential male-lead and says "Hey! Um. Mind if I come in? I think I found out something important about that vandal."

And I take off the safety chain before pulling the door open, just wide enough to let him in. But he keeps standing there and staring inside, somewhere in a spot, right behind me.

"Oh! Sorry! You have company. I'll see you at the cafe, tomorrow."

He might have noticed the empty wine bottle on the floor and Sophie's trench coat laying on my couch.

"No! Wait! Come in. This is more important!"

The smile on his face is blindingly bright. And, in a moment of confusion mixed with panic and hope, I can almost understand why Sophie is so fond of making those glorious mistakes.

• **Diary Entry** •

"You look pretty when your lips tremble like that!"

He would often say such despicable things. But why did we never say anything? Why did we never stop him?

"Don't be so shy! Everyone knows how much you like it. Just open wide and do as I say, okay? And then, you can taste it on your lips for the rest of the day." his voice had a desperate and suffocating quality. But, I never heard a response. The silence after his statements, felt stronger than his insistence.

Eventually, their frantic footsteps and the rustling of clothes had simmered away and I could hear something hitting the ground. I had assumed that someone was pushed down to the floor and it was abundantly clear that he was growing impatient.

"I'm doing you a favor. You should be thanking me." he sounded angry and his lackeys fanned the flame by calling the person a boring wanna-be who was desperate to be someone who mattered, to be one of them, but did not know how to have some fun.

I could hear it all. The door between us was too thin and their voices were just too loud. His insistence and demands always echoed in a room, in any room. And, as their manipulative words got harsher, the bathroom was slowly starting to stink.

With every inhale he savored, that followed a crackling sound of ash and amber, out came a smokey and suffocating exhale. The bathroom was just too small and it was getting harder to breathe.

I had to stay quite but I couldn't breathe, unless I gasped, unless I let the stink out and let some fresh air into my lungs. I tried so hard to control myself. But, my lungs couldn't take it anymore. So, after trying to hold it in, I inevitably coughed.

"Hey! Why don't you come out already? I know you keep hiding and watching me. You can help me teach her how to behave, right?"

The rustling of clothes and frantic footsteps, started echoing, again. And, I froze! I stood with my back pressed to the cold, tiled wall, while someone kicked the door open.

CHAPTER 3

TANGLED THREADS OF DESTINY

"Sit!"

I point toward the couch while moving the throw pillows. Sophie has a habit of piling them up, everywhere she sits. And, while it's easy to squish into a small space and sit next to her, I'm not sure if I can do the same with my business partner.

"Yes ma'am!"

Ma'am? Was that supposed to be funny? How old does he think I am?

"Do you say that to every woman you meet, at one in the morning?" I frown while setting aside the empty wine bottle.

"I'm sorry! I was just...!" he pauses and gulps.

Am I the one making him uncomfortable, after he showed up, unannounced? I didn't even have time to fix my hair. It must look like an abandoned bird's nest, like the one on my windowsill.

"Never mind. What did you find out?" I ask him while wiping the frown off my face.

He clears his throat and replies "The vandal seems to know some of our regular customers!".

"Regulars? Which ones?"

"Remember the two women who unusually sit outside, every Sunday morning, and drink at least 6 cups of coffee? The ones who always want privacy, and leave when someone sits too close to them?"

"Yeah! Double Caramel Cappuccino & Iced Latte With Extra Milk!"

"Yup! Them! Apparently, he is their husband!"

Did I hear that right? He said that a little too casually. I think it's a mistake. It must be. But I must ask. It's all too confusing to casually brush off as a slip of tongue.

"I'm sorry? Did you just say THEIR husband?"

"Mhm!" he is grinning. It's funny. He finds it amusing, again. I wonder what else excites him. It definitely isn't me. He just called me ma'am. And I feel like an old lady, thanks to this fine specimen of a man.

Oh! Wait! I need to tame my thoughts, for now. Because, he really just said THEIR husband. Oh my God! Is it that normal, for him? How is he grinning so casually? I can barely believe it. And I need to know more.

"WAIT! WHAT? HOW?" I yell, loud enough for Sophie to hear it from the apartment next door. But I'm sure she is loud enough on her own to notice it. God knows I can hear her from my bedroom. She is always so, so loud.

"It's…complicated! But I strongly believe that they can help us understand why that man is threatening us!" he replies with his doe eyes fixated on the trench coat.

"Uncomplicate it!" I insist while grabbing the coat and setting it aside, giving me room to slide closer to him.

I go through the stack of papers he has brought with him. And I find a bunch of pictures that look like grainy surveillance images from detective movies.

Who even is my business partner and what else is he capable of?

His eyes keep mapping my living room with every passing second. And I wonder if he looking for the owner of the trench coat.

Was Sophie right about him being interested in me?

"Where do I start?" he asks, innocently. His glittering eyes are now focused on the papers, as he methodically sets them down on my coffee table. His fingers gently pinch the corner of each picture, careful not to squeeze to hard and avoid forming wrinkles on the inked papers. It's fascinating to see his thumb gently smooth the corners that have curled from the edges. And I wonder what else he can do, methodically, with those dazzling digits.

No! Wait! I need to focus!

"Start from the beginning! Tell me everything!" I demand with a hint of excitement. But I'm mildly unsure of what excites me; the prospects of solving the vandal mystery or my proximity from my mysterious business partner. Our knees are inches apart. If I move just a little, or he shifts a little towards me, our knees might bump. And I wonder if it will give me goosebumps.

"Alright! Brace yourself!" he announces before his narration begins.

"Okay?" I dramatically grab my thighs to brace myself. And it makes him chuckles, softly.

Maybe I am funny enough for him. Maybe he does find something amusing about me.

As he narrates, his voice fills warmth into the walls. His words echoes, soothing the senses in a way that no one else does. I try to focus on what he is saying. But it's hard to not think of something else, something personal.

He is the first man, other than my brother, to have ever visited me at home. And it feels better than being the only one bringing this place to life. But I pull myself out of my dreamy thoughts and focus on what he is saying.

"Basically, the man was already married when he met someone else, during a work trip. They seemed to get along and he somehow hid his infidelity from his wife, long enough for things to get serious with this other woman. At some point, the man could not keep up with his double life anymore, and he did some messed up things to find a way out. But I'm not sure what happened after that.

His two wives…" he pauses to chuckle, with a hint of embarrassment, before he continues.

"The two women decided to run away from him, together, for some reason, and they started a new life here. He must have tracked them down and subsequently found out about our cafe. But that's all I know, so far."

He looks through the papers and adds "Oh and apparently the women have been raising two kids together. Twins, a boy and a girl. But I do not know from whom and how the twins come into the picture. This is all I could find out, so far!".

He takes a deep breath and sinks into the couch. Maybe storytelling, fictional or factual, is not as easy as some people may think. It's tiring and thankless. He did a good job! Maybe I should tell him that. He managed to find out a lot of useful information.

"This is great! You did great, Jay! I'll share these with Sophie. She knows someone in the local PD. I'm sure they can help us out."

"Already shared everything with the PD in our block. I know their ace detective. We practically grew up together. He has always been an ace at everything so the case is in his capable hands. And he has personally assured us that he will help us track down this man. And yes, I have already emailed all the necessary information to Sophie as well. I know that you trust her with everything. She's good at what she does."

He smiles! And it feels sincere.

"Oh and I've texted my detective friend's number to her, our cafe staff and, of course, you! All of us can contact him, anytime. It will be best to keep him in loop regarding this whole situation, especially if we notice something suspicious around us. It's better to be safe and prepared in such cases."

"Are you always like this?" I ask while heading towards the kitchen to fetch a glass of water for him.

"Like what?" he questions back, with his eye fixated on the trench coat again, as he slowly follows me and stands with his back to the refrigerator.

I seriously hope that he does not lean back and mess up my methodical arrangement.

"Jack of all trade?" I hand him the glass.

He chugs down the water and sets the glass inside the sink. Does he have to be so well mannered? It's getting harder to not like him anymore.

My eyes are still fixated on the glass in the sink when he asks "What were you planning on baking?".

And I turn around, only to see him glaring at the box of all-purpose flour, that is still sitting on my kitchen counter.

"Shouldn't you be sleeping by now? It's too late to bake, unless you're planning on skipping work in the morning." he smirks.

Why does everyone keep smirking?

"Alright! Go home! The cafe needs you more than it needs me. And you need to sleep." I try pulling him towards the door. But, he resists.

Why is he so strong? He is barely making any effort and I can barely move him.

"My home is too far away. Can't I just sleep on your couch? I don't snore! Promise! I'll not bother you!" he pleads with his big doe eyes, looking helplessly at me. And what am I supposed to do? Kick him out?

"Fine! But you're baking a cake before you leave!"

"Yes, ma'am! F**k! Sorry!" he smacks his forehead before running to the couch and hiding his face into one of the cushions. If I was drunk, I'd call him a puppy.

"Do you need to use the bathroom?" I ask while pointing at the door down the hall.

"Maybe later? Your couch is so comfy!" he curls into a ball and hugs a cushion, plastering it to his check.

And that's the last adorable thing he does before dozing off, almost instantly, once I double lock my front door and turn off the lights.

But he did lie about one thing. He does snore, a lot. And yet, I get enough sleep, even with how loud he is. Maybe I just need someone around to feel safe enough to get some quality sleep, even in my own apartment.

Thankfully, I wake up to a the smell of freshly baked cupcakes and the sounds of Sophie noisily munching on them. I can even hear Jay laughing about her satisfied expressions. He calls it "her bedroom face" and she instantly agrees, with a big bite of cake, still in her mouth.

My best friend, getting along with someone other than me, is shocking and equally comforting.

• *Diary Entry* •

"You have done this before, haven't you?" his question had echoed in the bathroom while one of his lackeys dragged me out of the stall. But, I had nothing to say. And, it was hard to look at the person, someone I adored, with her knees glued to the ground. So, my eyes remained glued to the floor.

"You always hide and watch, every time I find myself a new play thing. You are always hiding behind boxes and doorways, sneaking up on me, huh? Is this thrilling for you? Does this make you feel things? Wouldn't it be better if you did something instead of being a silent spectator? You've seen enough! You know she likes it. They all do!"

He kept talking, kept assuming. And I wondered if his words suppressed our instincts. I wondered if his insistence made us believe that he did nothing wrong. But, deep down, I knew it was all wrong.

I had looked up for a second and glanced into her eyes, hoping to see some of the usual sparkle. Her eyes always had a shade of kindness in them. But, that shine had disappeared into the darkness.

All I could see was discomfort, distrust and disgust.

A rogue tear had painted a saline streak across her cheek. The droplet was sparkling on the edge of her jawline, shaking from the force of her clenching jaw and twitching lips.

"Let me explain something to you, real quick!" he had said before pulling me closer. The collar of my shirt was bunched up in his fist and the air was struggling to find it's way into my lungs.

"Man up and make her do it. And, I promise, I'll let her leave. Okay?" he instructed, with his eyes fixed on her, and mine followed his hungry gaze.

A lit cigarette dangled dangerously between her trembling lips. It's flame was inching closer and closer to the collar of her polyester shirt.

CHAPTER 4

BUCKLE UP

It was just like any other rainy day. The low-lying areas were closing up by noon. Some shops across the intersection, were ankle deep in water. Most people were either in their office or at home, away from the fury of the thundering skies.

Our cafe was practically empty, even when our neighborhood was not badly effected by the rains. Everyone was used to seeing such days during the wet season. And I usually spent such a slow, rainy day, with Sophie. So, we were planning on meeting, right after she was done with a work emergency.

One minute, I was on a call with her, talking about her assistant who messed up and scheduled a house viewing, while it was raining cats and dogs. She was saying that she would drop by, right after she was done showing an apartment to a new client. And the next minute, I heard her screaming before she hung up.

"Something happened to Sophie! I have to go!" I yell while grabbing my raincoat. The obnoxious thing is just too tight. But it's pouring outside and I will soak like a sponge.

"Where are you going? Do you even know where she is, right now?" Jay yells back while grabbing his windbreaker jacket and his car keys. He will get drenched in the rain if he walk around in that flimsy thing. But I do not have time to worry about him, not when Sophie is in danger.

"Send everyone home. Close the cafe! It's not safe today! And lock up before you go!" he instructs Tanya, from the parking lot, before pulling out his car and driving up to me.

"Hop in!" he suggests while I'm frantically wandering the streets, looking for a cab. The rain keeps intensifying and I wipe my face with the back of my palm. But I can't see a cab or even another car on the street. So, I decide to hop in.

"Where was she, when you called? Do you have her location?" he asks, right after I close the door.

"I have her last drop location, from the ride sharing app. She has added me as her emergency contact." I mentally thank the stars for the day when we decide to add each other as our emergency contact. It has made it easier for us to keep an eye on each other's safety.

"Great! Where is it?" Jay asks, a little urgently.

"It's somewhere around that newest redevelopment cluster, right next to the community center. She was about to meet a potential buyer."

"Alright! Buckle up!" he instruct and I follow. There is no point risking our safety while looking for her.

The seat belt is suffocating me, every time we stop at a red light, not because it's uncomfortable but because I'm anxious. And I hope she's okay.

She isn't picking up my calls anymore.

"Take the next right and pull over, somewhere you can park. She must be here! She has to be!." I instruct and Jay takes a sharp turn. His urgency is evident. Maybe I was wrong to doubt him around the time of the vandalism. Maybe he isn't as self centered as he seems.

"Found a spot!" he parks into an empty spot near a deli that seems to have closed up for good.

"There! That's the building!" I point at the tall, newly renovated structure, as I hop out of the car. The water splashes and gets inside my shoes when I step out of the car.

But I do not have time to worry about myself. I need to find Sophie. She must be here, somewhere. I remember hearing sounds of rain and cars passing by, before she hung up. She might still be out in the rain, alone, drenched. And I need to find her, fast!

"Sophie! Sophie!"

I keep yelling her name as I run into the alley next to the apartment building. It's just instincts, or maybe a fear driven assumption. And I keep running until I reach the end of the alley. But I can't find her.

Jay follows me while screaming something. But I can barely focus on his words enough to understand them. So I keep running down the block, until I notice a familiar trench coat.

It's her! It's my Sophie. She's hurt and isn't moving.

"Hey! Hey! I'm here! Sophie! I'm here!" I lift her head and pull her onto my lap.

She is cold, so cold.

"Wake up! I'm here! Look at me! What were you doing here, all by yourself? Didn't I tell you to take someone with you, when you meet a new buyer? Come on! Get up!" I keep screaming and sobbing while Jay calls for help.

She is cold, so cold!

An ambulance arrives, soon enough, and we are rushed to the nearest ER. Jay drives behind the ambulance while I ride with Sophie. Her cold hand, wrapped in my palm, keeps shaking and twitching. And, in a few minutes, we are wheeled into the ER.

The doctors who run her tests, decide to keep her overnight, for observation. So, I decide to call her ex and inform him about the incident. There are detectives and uniformed officers surrounding Sophie's private room, by the time I've made a few important calls.

When she is conscious enough and out of her shocked state of mind, a detective calmly asks "Was it him?" while showing her a picture of the vandal that we had to deal with. And all she does is nod.

"You can't stay at your place after you are discharged. And you..." the detective swings his gaze from Sophie and focuses on me, before he adds "...you too can not stay at home, until we have located this lunatic! Where else can you stay?".

"A hotel? Sophie and I can stay together." I hold her hand and feel the warmth. It's comforting. She is okay. She is here. And that's all that matters.

But I notice Jay, with his furrowed brows, pressing his lips and grinding his teeth. His drenched clothes and soaked shoes have left a small puddle of water under his feet. And I wonder if he is mad at me for not caring about him as much as I care about Sophie.

"I'm not sure if that's a good idea!" the detective frowns.

And Jay adds "Anyone can easily sneak into a hotel room. I don't think it's safe to stay in an unknown environment, right now.".

It's oddly comforting to see him reacting like this. And I wonder if he really care about me or if it's just his nature to care about everyone around him.

"Where is she? Where is she?" we can hear a familiar voice, yelling outside the room.

It turns out to be Sophie's ex, frantically babbling at the reception and looking for her. And Jay quickly calms him before bringing him into her room.

"We will give you some privacy!" Jay suggests, as he grabs my hand and pulls me out of the room. Even the detectives decide to come back later, when Sophie is feeling a little better.

And, as I get pulled out of the room and we walk towards an empty corridor, all I can do is focus on how tightly Jay grips my wrist. Is he worried about me? Or is he just worried about his business partner and his business itself?

Do I mean anything to him?

We stop at the end of the hallway and Jay turns to face me. His grasp slightly loosens but he does not let go of my wrist. His usually, bright eyes, seem tired and restless. I know that he has something to say, but he keeps staring at me for a moment before he clears his throat and starts talking.

"You need to change! You're soaking wet. And that raincoat is nothing but a plastic contraption that's suffocating you. Let me take you to your place so that you can change and grab your things. You're coming home with me, tonight!"

"I'll be fine! Sophie can stay with her ex in his family home, after she gets discharged. She will be safe there. And hotels are safer than you think!"

"Nonetheless, I'll feel better if you stay at my place. It's far from the city and practically off-grid. That lunatic can not track you there!" Jay insists as he loosens his grip on my wrist until he reluctantly let's go.

"And what will you do? Where will you stay?" I joke, of course.

What else am I supposed to say? That I'm uncomfortable? That I've never stayed at a man's house before? That I think he is being too generous, or too sly? Or that I want him to keep holding my hand, even if it hurts a little.

"I'll stay in a hotel if you want the place, all to yourself. There is one, just a few miles from my place. It's small and cozy. I've been there before."

"I was kidding! I can't possibly force you to let me stay. This is not your problem to deal with. Whatever the man wants from me is probably on me, somehow. Maybe I offend him when he was lurking around our neighborhood!"

"Lurking?" Jay furrowed his brows. I don't think I've ever seen him look so angry.

"Why did you not tell me that he has been lurking around your home?" he is grinding his teeth again.

"Because I did not want to bother you. You're already doing more than you need to!"

"That's it! Let's go! Grab your stuff! I'm taking you home, right now!" he grabs my hand again before dragging me back towards Sophie's room. It's funny! His grip is tighter now but it feels better, warmer.

I say a quick goodbye to Sophie, who is tucked into her ex's arms. And I know him enough to know that he will keep her safe. It's a relief to say the least.

"I'll go get the car! See you outside!" Jay says, before rushing out of the room. His wet shoes, make a squeaking sound, as he runs down the hallway that leads to the exit. And I keep wondering why the squeaky steps sound so comforting.

Once I've double checked to make sure that Sophie will be safe in her room, I give my number to the officers who are stationed outside her room, just in case they need to contact me. But I hope that they don't. I hope we would never have to experience something like this, ever again.

"Stay safe, okay?" Sophie mumbles, as I wave at her for one last time, before I absolutely must leave. And I follow Jay's wet footstep, that are being mopped dry, as I walk down the hallway.

When I'm finally outside the ER wing, I quickly spot Jay and his car in the parking lot. There is a tall man inside a dark booth who is handing Jay the receipt. And Jay, who is stuffing his wallet back into the back pocket of his fitted pants, is practically rushing into his car before promptly driving towards me.

I want to hold him. I want to tell him that I'm okay and we are okay. I want him to know that he does not need to worry so much. Because, I know how suffocating it must be for him to worry about everyone in his life.

Isn't he done being suffocated over someone else's problems?

When Jay pulls over and asks me to get in, I peel off my raincoat and throw it into a trashcan nearby. Because, I am certainly done being suffocated.

We quickly drop by my apartment and I change into a dry set of clothes. But, there isn't much time to relish the warm feeling from the dry fabric. My damp shoes come off my swollen feet with a little effort, right before I grab a pair of comfort sneakers and look for the things that I need.

As I grab my journal and a new pack of sticky notes from my night stand, my pen suddenly decides to rolls away from me. It falls into the gap between my bed and the absurdly heavy bedside table. And, I remind myself that Jay must definitely have a spare pen at home. So, instead of wedging my hand into the insufficient gap, I hurry back to my wardrobe and grab my emergency travel bag.

Jay keeps nervously walking up and down the corridor, refusing to come in and wipe himself off. He seems genuinely worried and I keep wondering if he really cares so much about me, or if he is just used to being considerate.

"Got what you need?" he asks and I nod while locking the door.

As we wait for the elevator, I looking around my usually dim corridor. And somehow, it seems brighter than usual. So, I wonder if loneliness can makes a place look more unsettling than usual.

"Let's go!" Jay announces when the elevator finally arrives. And we step in, together. His damp shoulder bumps into mine and leaves a wet patch in it's wake.

"Thanks for helping us!" I look towards Jay and hand him a dry towel. He has been soaking wet and running around, for us, without caring for his own well-being. It feels unnecessarily selfless!

"Thanks...for this!" Jay smiles, brightly and wholeheartedly, before he wipes his face and dries his hair.

The elevator dings again when it reaches the basement. And, we step into the dimly lit parking area. I never dared entering the basement on my own. But, for some reason, the basement seems harmless in Jay's presence.

"Are there any security cameras in this parking lot?" Jay ask and I shake my head. There's barely enough light in the common areas across the premises. And the building manager is not keen on addressing our concerns, unless everyone votes on it.

"If you ask for my option, I think you should avoid coming here, alone." Jay suggests while looking for his car in a sea of metal on wheels. And, when I spot it, shining under a surprisingly bright ceiling light, I wonder if the light is brighter or my observation is sharper for some reason.

As we approach his car, he presses a button that softly opens the trunk. And I sincerely hope that he has a dry shirt or something useful in there.

"Just a second!" he says while pulling out a t-shirt from inside a bag. A gym bag, perhaps. That could explain why he is so freakishly strong.

"Turn around!" he smiles, mischievously, while taking off his wet jacket. And I turn. But, I'm immediately facing a huge, round mirror, the kind that's in every parking lot to help you navigate safely.

Unintentionally, at first, but I keep watching and admiring the view. I can see his back, flexing, as he peels off his wet shirt and throws it into the trunk, right next to the wet jacket. But I quickly look away by the time he proceeds to wear his dry t-shirt.

It's embarrassing! I usually do not look at men as an object of desire. Their bodies usually do not attract me. But, maybe it's Jay. Maybe it's the way he cares, that makes him look a little appealing, especially at this point in time.

Or maybe it's just because he looks gorgeous. His shirts never really hide his broad shoulders or his tiny waist.

How is he so beautiful and equally kind?

"All done! Come on! Let's go home!" he closes the trunk of his car and quickly opens the passenger side door for me. How chivalrous!

How is he even real?

The drive is long and his home seems way too far away. And I understand why he slept on my couch that night. This feels like a brutal daily commute.

"I forgot to tell you something!" he suddenly breaks the silence and sneaks a look towards me before focusing on the road again.

"Yeah! What is it?" I ask.

"Those two women, our regulars? Remember the kids that they were raising?"

"Mhm!"

"There's a small change that I know them."

"Wait! What? How?" I question him while looking at his bright eyes that are glittering again.

"I think we went to the same school for a while. But I'm not sure. So I'm having someone look into it. Apparently the man made a lot of money before he messed up his life, downsized and moved away with his first wife and the twins. But he got incredibly abusive and resentful. And that other woman? She helped his wife and kids run away and relocate." Jay pauses and checks his rear view mirror. There is a sense of worry, dimming the shine in his eyes, just for a second, until he hides it away.

I wonder what is going on in his mind.

"It seems like they have been through a lot. Maybe there is more to this whole story than we know, so far. Maybe we will understand better, eventually." I try to assume him that he does not need to worry, alone, chasing pain while looking for answers.

"True! But, honestly, I'm still not sure why that other women moved with them, or why his first wife trusted her, more than she trusted her cheating husband, or her own birth family. I'll never understand how someone's birth family can simply ignore and abandon their child, or their grand children." Jay sighs.

There isn't any right way of saying it, but I think I am starting to understand the relationship between those two women. Maybe they have what Sophie and I do; a friendship of convenience and a bond strengthened through misery.

I look outside the window as we pass diners and motels near the city limit. It's gloomy, even when the rain has stopped and the roads aren't filled with hasty, honking cars anymore.

"Hey, Jay?"

"Hmmm?"

"I think I should stay only for the night and then move to the hotel that you were talking about. It must be safe if someone like you chose to stay."

"Yeah, safe for me. I can box. You're a marshmallow with feelings. I need to protect you!" he chuckles.

"Did you just call me a marshmallow?"

"I did! Because, I think you're very sweet!"

Why is he being so cute?

"Fine! I'll stay for a few days, until this settle. What did your detective friend say to you before he left?"

"He thinks we should lay low for at least a week!"

"Alright! I'll stay for a week. But only if you stay with me. Marshmallows need protection, I guess!" I laugh.

And Jay, with his glittering eyes and twitching lips, hides a smile and eats his words, until we reach the tall walls of his compound.

Today's mood was terrible, awful, stressful. But he managed to turn it into a bitter-sweet kind of day.

Maybe I can survive without Sophie, if she ever chooses to forget me and move on with her life. Maybe I'll have him, right here, by my side, even if it's just as a dedicated business partner.

"Welcome home!" he says, as he presses a button on his dashboard. And his front gates start to part, letting the iron barrier make way for an unexpected view ahead.

"I was expecting a small, off-grid house with a couple of rocking chairs, and a little garden." I activate my coping mechanism, because, this is all too much. I'm not sure how else to express my disbelief. Humor is all I can think of.

How much money does he have?

"Well, I do have recliners in my backyard, right by the pool. And I can always order us a couple of rocking chairs, if that's what you want!" he smiles at me after parking in his driveway. His eyes rock back and forth between my oily nose and chapped lips. And that reminds me that I forgot to bring my lip balm.

"Shall we?" he asks before hopping out of the car and opening my side of the door. And he extends his hand to hold my bag, even before I can fully process the fact that a man just opened the door for me, for the second time, in a single day.

How can he possibly be real?

"Um! Yeah! Let's go see if two people can even fit in this house." I nervously chuckle, expecting a laugh or maybe even a look of disappointment at my joke.

Instead, he simply winks and says "We might have to share a bed!".

• *Diary Entry* •

It was just a regular cigarette. There was nothing different about it. Almost everyone smoked in the dorms and campus hideouts.

But, why did he always do that?

Why was he incapable of taking NO for an answer? Why did he have to force her to smoke? Why did he have to force that exchange student to drink during that one department party for seniors? And why did he have to use his family name as a warning? Did any of them deserve to be threatened and manipulated?

She did not deserve to be treated this way! None of them deserved it. But, I was too scared. His family name was stronger than mine. He had already proven it when I tried stopping him from bullying someone in school, just a few years ago. We had grown up together. But, he made me question if I even belonged in a World that cherished and celebrated him.

I did not have it in me to be beaten up for being a hero, again. I knew my family would be disappointed if I tried acting like a savior, again. So, I did what I thought was the right thing to do.

I freed my collar from his grip before pushing him and his lackeys aside. And, I ran, as fast as I could.
I left her behind with that monster and, I ran.

There were footsteps behind me for a while. But, I raced up the stairs and rushed out of the building. The smoke was slowly pushed out of my lungs. My heart was racing, knowing very well that, what I did, was no better than what he was doing to her.

But, I could finally breathe again.

CHAPTER 5

FORTRESS

"You'll be safe here, I promise!" Jay assures me, as we walk into the house. There are no names on his front door but, the address reads ONE FOUR THREE in bold letters embossed on a metal surface.

Jay talks about his security system that has cameras across the compound and a live feed on his phone. He tilts the screen towards me and tells me about every blind spot that I need to avoid, in case I decide to go out for some fresh air.

"I'll get you access for the live feed, so you can keep tabs from your phone, while you stay." he smiles as he takes off his squeaky, wet shoes.

I look around and nod while stepping out of my sneakers. It's been a long, overwhelming day. And we still have to deal with a lot, now that I've been whisked away from my apartment, my life and my Sophie.

I wonder how she's doing, right now. I hope she is okay. And I hope that the detectives can find that man sooner than he finds us, again. And frankly, I can't even begin to imagine what kind of person Jay is and why is he so willing to help us.

Sophie was right! He truly seems to have it all. And yet, he is getting his own hands dirty in a strange situation like this.

Is it because he feels guilty about something? Did something in his past, shape him into the man he has become, in this phase of life? I wonder if he will ever open up to me. But, it would be nice to know him, maybe just a little better than I do, right now.

"Here's your room!" he guides me to what looks like a guest room that overlooks the pool. He then shows me around and points at everything he think I may need. The room has virtually everything a house guest may need. And it has a gorgeous bathroom attached to it.

The place looks massive. There is a bed, big enough to fit half a dozen regular-sized women who eat nothing but salads. There is a cozy couch, right next to the big window that overlooks the pool. And it makes me want to sit there and look outside, for the rest of the night. The view must be amazing. It's getting dark and the sky looks clearer than it does in the city.

I keep looking around as he shows me everything he thinks I may need. Thankfully, there's an orange scented lip balm on the night stand, right next to some orange scented skin care products. And I wonder if he likes the taste of artificial orange flavoring.

Does he have to be so methodical and well preparing, all the time? It makes him unnecessarily attractive to say the least. And I almost worry why he is so kind to me because, Sophie was right! He truly seems to have it all. Then why would he ever need me in his life, or his business?

My thoughts almost dampen his voice until I pull back my attention and focus on him.

"...cold at night! So make sure you sleep with the blanket on. And remember, you can just pick up the landline and dial seven for my bedroom, in case you don't want to get out of the covers." he chuckles.

"Sounds fancy but okay!" I smile, nervously.

"I'm serious! Call me, anytime you need anything. Do not hesitate, okay? And let me know what you eat, so I can cook something for us."

He sounds like a dream. Why is he doing all this? I wonder if I'm special or if he is just used to being kind to everyone.

"I'll be fine! Thank you! And I'm not a picky eater. I'm just mildly allergic to dairy. Everything else is fine."

He holds in a laugh and says "It seems like an extremely inconvenient allergy for a cafe owner!".

"It's not that inconvenient, with you around! I mean, you do make great alternative recipes, even for our dairy intolerant customers!" I want to smack my head. But, I try smiling and wish that he could read my mind.

Why can't I just say what I want to say?

It's a relief to see his face softens again as he asks "Would you like to borrow something from my wardrobe?".

And then, I remember! I did not grab the right clothes to wear, before leaving my apartment in a rush. All I have in my bag, are some daily essential, a toothbrush, a few underwear, some mismatched socks, a few long t-shirts that I usually wear when I sleep, and my wallet with a nearly maxed out credit card. Those are things that practically live inside the bag for emergencies or for when I have a sleepover at Sophie's.

Is sleepover even the right word at our age?

"I think I can manage for the night. But I'll have to get some more clothes from my apartment, tomorrow! I definitely did not pack enough for a week. Do you get any kind of cab service around here?"

"Don't worry! I'll get someone to drop by your apartment and bring some clothes from your wardrobe, if that's okay with you. And, until then, feel free to borrow anything you like, from my wardrobe." he says while pointing at a room down the hall.

I'm assuming that it's his bedroom because, it's the only room with larger than usual doors. In fact, the room has sliding doors, the kind I used to love playing with, when I was little. It reminds me of some of my fondest childhood memories. My grandpa had doors like those in the family home.

I miss him.

sigh

"I'll be fine in these, for now!" I point at what I'm wearing. But, to be honest, I wish I could change into something more comfortable. The long t-shirts are not long enough for a night in my business partner's ridiculously lavish house. I may have seen the reflection of his back but I refuse to show him the folds of my things.

"Are you sure? I do have new clothes! You don't have to wear something old that smell like me!" he laughs.

It's not like I don't want to smell like him. But, he needs to know why I can't wear his clothes. It's embarrassing but he deserves to know.

"I don't think your clothes will fit me!" I shine a blinding light on the elephant in the room, by pointing at his tiny waist.

But, instead of laughing or making a fuss about it, he runs to his room and comes back with an oversized t-shirt along with a pair of baggy pants.

"These are new! I just bought them, last week. They are extremely comfortable and hypoallergenic. And don't worry, they don't smell like me, at all!" his lips gently curl up into a shy smile.

Honestly, he always smells like vanilla and coffee. I would not mind smelling like a breakfast treat. All I smell like is stress and disappointment. And I desperately need a hug right now.

Does neediness have a smell?

"Thank you! I'll buy you a new pair."

"That's fine! I just want you to be comfortable here."

He walks away and closes the door behind him, and I'm left alone in his guest room for the next hour and a half. It takes me a while to shower and get ready because his bathroom is just that cozy. It feels impossible to step out of the serene shower.

After a while, I hear a series of knocks on the door. And, when I open it, he leans closer and says "Dinner is ready!".

Did I hit my head on my way here?
Am I hallucinating, right now?
Is any of this even real?

"You did not have to do all this!" I can barely form a sentence. No one has ever cooked for me before.

This is overwhelming.

"Ah! Come on! You're my guest. I must take care of you. You let me sleep on your couch. That was the best sleep I had in years. This is to thank you for that. Come on now! Let's eat before it gets cold!"

During dinner, we talk about the Sophie situation, about the twins, and about how he got into the business of baking and brewing for a living. Apparently, his mom taught him how to bake and his dad always encouraged him to do anything constructive and creative he wanted with his life.

Maybe this is what it looks like, growing up in a healthy environment. Maybe that's why he looks so beautiful.

Peace of mind looks beautiful on everyone.

"Give me a week. I promise I'll bring normalcy back to your life!" his voice almost echoes in the hall as we walk back to my room after dinner.

My room?
Did I just say my room?

This is too good for me to get comfortable with. It's not something I can deserve in a million years. I don't even know what normalcy is. All this is beyond my imagination. All of him is beyond my imagination.

"Normalcy? I don't think my life has ever been normal in any way!" I laugh to lighten my statement.

"Maybe that's a good thing!" he leans on the doorframe when we reach the guest room.

"I think, if anyone can fix this situation, it's you, Jay! Clearly, you know something we don't. And you can tell me about it when you're ready to share. I'll just trust you and stay here for a week. But only if you let me pay you back, somehow!"

"I know how you can pay me back!" he smirks.

It's confusing. I already have mixed feelings.

"Yeah? And how's that?" I ask.

But he leans closer and closer until he rests his forehead on my shoulder and asks "Can I sleep here, with you? I find sleep to be oddly comforting, when you are around.".

"Um...sure? I can sleep on the couch. You take the bed, okay?" I'm unable to move. His head is still resting on my shoulder. But, it feels warm and fuzzy.

"I meant, I could take the couch. Or, maybe, we can both take the bed and I can build a pillow fort between us?" he asks when he finally lifts his head off me.

And suddenly, my shoulder feels cold again. I miss the weight on me. I miss the warmth. I miss him. It's illogical! He is standing right in front of me. And I still miss him. I miss his touch. So, I cave.

"Pillows, huh? How many?" I ask him while looking at the bed. It's definitely big enough for the three of us; him, his pillow fort and my slightly excited self.

But, before I can get a reply, he is running back to his bedroom and coming back with a bunch of pillows, in several shapes and sizes.

He sets them in the middle of the bed and draws a soft, fluffy line between our sides of the bed.

This is crazy! I was suspecting him, a few weeks ago, and now I'm agreeing to share a bed with him.

"Is this good enough?" he asks and I nod. Because, honestly, it's all so innocent and sweet. I missed this more than I missed being in a relationship or even dating anyone. Sleeping together, like this? This is almost exactly what I want, most of the time. Maybe just with fewer pillow? But, for now, that looks like the right amount of fluff between us.

The rest of the night passes fast between random conversations and fixing the wall of pillow. And before I realize, I doze off next to him.

When I wake up, early next morning, I see Jay sleeping with a peaceful expression on his face. It's funny that he did not snore at all, throughout the night. Maybe he was telling the truth. Maybe my couch made him snore when he slept at my place.

His arm has crossed the wall of pillows and is resting next to mine. I wonder if we were holding hands last night, in our sleep. I don't remember but it feels oddly comforting to think about it.

Today's mood is already looking bright, filled with comfort and hope.

I grab my phone and check my messages. Sophie will be discharged in a few hours and her ex has made all the necessary arrangements for them to stay in his family home, at least until the matter is truly settled. I want to call her but I wait, remembering that she must be asleep.

Instead of waking her up and potentially worrying her, I call our staff at the cafe, letting them know that we might be coming in late. But they insisted that we stay back where it's safe, suggesting that they can handle a slow weekday on their own. However, I advise them to call us, in case they need any help. And I instruct them to close up and leave, if they see the lunatic lurking around.

Money is important but so is life. The safety of our staff and customers, has and always will be, our first priority. The call runs long as my over-thinking keeps making up scenarios and giving them instructions on how to handle it. And maybe, the long call woke him up because, Jay is stirring and slowly waking up.

He retreats his arm and smile with his eyes barely open. It's enchanting. How can someone, so sleepy, look so good, at such an early hour?

"Did I wake you up?" I asks and he shakes his head.

"I usually wake up at this time!" his voice sounds deeper than usual. It's intoxicating.

Soon enough, he makes breakfast for us, just like that one time he made cupcakes for Sophie. But he doesn't comment on the faces I make while eating. He just looks at me, with a gentle, confusing smile. And I wonder what he thinks of me when he isn't seeing me as a business partner or a temporary house guest.

Jay decided to stay home for the day. He keeps making calls and stays busy on his phone. And I just walk around, absorbing the house that looks twice as big in the day as it did at night.

I even manage to make lunch for us from everything I can recognize in his refrigerator. My unrefined palate can not recognize half the fresh produce and most of the ingredients in his cabinet. My refrigerator is usually filled with ingredients for sandwiches and toaster-oven pizzas.

Maybe I got too used to eating for survival, instead of eating to savor a comforting meal.

Jay seems different after lunch. Maybe I shocked him with my cooking skills. But he keeps smiling, keeps gravitating towards me and keeps eating his words before he can share what's on his mind. Or maybe I did not cook enough and he is still hungry.

I still can't fully understand him. But this is nice! Whatever this is, it's comforting me. And I'm thankful for all that he is doing for me, for us, and for our business.

"Hey, Jay?" I ask while we make dinner together.

"Yeah?"

"How's your schedule for tomorrow?"

"I think I should go to the cafe. They probably need me. You still need to stay here. This is the safest place for you, for now. There are cameras around the compound, a patrol van that is always driving by, and my people are just a call away."

"Hmmm! You're right. The cafe needs you more than it needs me, at least for now."

The chopping sound suddenly pauses and I feel his fingers gently wrapping around my wrist. His thumb gently swiping over my pulse point and I can barely focus on what he says next.

"The cafe needs you as much as it needs me. It's your business as much as it is mine. But, for now, we all need you to be safe, so you can come back and continue your creative magic. I can bake all I want but nothing is the same without you!". He gently lets go of my hand and resume chopping the vegetables.

And deep down, I'm screaming, celebrating. I want him to keep holding me. But just like him, I eat my own words and simmer my smile before I simmer the pot in front of me. Thank God for the steam. My face must be flushed right now.

After dinner, we decide to rest outside, by the pool, while looking at the stars. He was right about the recliners. It gives the best views of the skies.

This house is far enough from the city for the night to be less blurred out by artificial lights. And the stars seem to twinkle a lot brighter. It's magical.

"Hey, Jay?"

"Yeah?"

"Thank you!"

"For what?" he asks after turning to face me.

But I keep looking at the stars. I might loose my calm if I look at him right now. His doe eyes shine like a million stars that have descended on Earth.

"For making room for me, in your business!"

He smiles and looks back at the sky before he replies "Our business! And thank you for trusting me!".

I want to say more, so much more. But I can manage to add just one more line. Just one more thought manages to roll off my lips.

"And thank you for making room for me in your home!" I keep looking at the stars, hoping to not freak out, if he looks at me a little too fondly. And he does. And yes, I do freak out. I freeze and keep looking away. My courage only allows me to see him from the corner of my eye.

And he keeps staring at me, affectionately. But I feel like he holds back more than he should. I can see his lips twitch and part just a little before pressing back, seeking silence. I wonder what was on his mind. Maybe, in another world, in another universe, he said something that I wanted to hear.

We decide to sleep early. The next morning will have to be a regular morning for him. He has to get some rest. And I have to get some privacy, to scream my feelings into a pillow. So we sleep in separate beds.

I do remind him to come to my room, if he has trouble smelling. But he says that he needs me to be comfortable and reminds me to call him if I need something.

I agree to call if I need anything. But what could I possibly need? A hug, maybe? Wouldn't that be a ridiculous request?

After we have said our good nights and I have tucked myself under the covers, I look at the other side of the enormous bed. It feels empty without the dozen pillows and a sweet, affectionate man, right next to me.

• *Diary Entry* •

I never expected to meet her again. It was highly unlikely for us to cross paths after what happened in that basement. I had stopped seeing her around campus and I assumed that she left. They always left after any such incident.

But, I always dreaded the possibilities.

She had seen my face, that day. She knew who I was. And, I wonder what would happen if I ever bumped into her. What if she confronted me? What if she blamed everyone who turned a blind eye? Or, what if she was actively looking for me?

That is exactly why I decided to leave, right after I graduated. It made no sense to keep living among those people anymore. I never fit in. I was almost invisible. And no one would even notice if I left that world behind.

Eventually, I mustered the courage to move to another city, in hopes of living without the shadows of my past and the weight of my family name. I just wanted a normal life, a normal job and maybe even a normal relationship, someday.

But, I kept bumping into women who reminded me of her. Women who looked like her, dressed like her, walked like her or even talked like her.

Maybe it was life's way of tormenting me. Or maybe it was life's way of reminding me that it was never too late to make amends.

I left her there, with them, all alone. There was no one else who knew where she was on that fateful day. It was just him, his lackeys and me, who knew what was happening to her. But, I left her there and ran away, like a coward.

I told myself that, no matter how horrible, it was just a cigarette. I told myself that, all she had to do was let him watch her smoke. And then, he would let her go. He was a monster but also a man of his words.

I really tried to convince myself that I was not as bad as they were. But, was I any good? Or, was I worse?

And soon, I realized that it was time to stop running away and start making amends, even if it was someone I did not hurt, even if it was someone I did not know. The only way to repent, was to make amends, until I met her again and asked for her forgiveness.

That lead me to start working for a special branch of the local PD. We worked as consultants for a variety of cases throughout the precinct. It was our duty to look for pattern and help solve cold cases. And, I hoped for it to help me redeem myself, until I could ask for her forgiveness.

CHAPTER 6

THE WHOLE TRUTH

Happiness can make it harder to grasp the concept of time.

Some moments feel like an eternity, like the day when I woke up next to Jay and his hand was gently wrapped around my wrist. He was still on the floor, right where he was before I fell asleep in the middle of our conversation.

"I don't want to hog your bed!" he had said before grabbing a blanket, wrapping himself like a burrito and sitting on the floor next to my bed.

My bed.

I was restless and he assured that he would stay, until I fell asleep. I had assumed that he would leave, eventually. But, he never did.

His head was awkwardly resting on the mattress and his hair tickled me awake before the clock did. And I looked at him for what felt like hours. But, it must have been a few minutes before the alarm rang and he woke up, smiling like the bright summer sun that was peaking from the horizon.

Some moment remind us that time is flying away before we can enjoy the beautiful changes in life.

Sophie decided to take the ultimate next step when she realized that, no one can have her back, the way her ex does.

And she officially moved in with him. Even her furniture and fixtures left her penthouse and crowded his side of the family home.

Her ex is still paying for the apartment in my building and planning on holding on to it, for now. It would be hard to get a better place than that, in case Sophie dumps him, again.

I love Sophie but even I think that it's a very wise decision. We both know that my best friend is an emotionally volatile volcano with deep pockets. She can afford to do anything on an impulse.

"I wish you were here, right now!" Sophie had said over the phone while waiting for the moving truck to arrive. And I genuinely wished that I was there, right by her side. But, Jay insisted that I stayed under the radar until the dust settled and we were all safe again. He did not want the attacker to follow me again and find out where Sophie had moved to. And I couldn't find any loopholes in his logic.

"I'll visit you, soon!" I assured Sophie before we started joking about the things that we would do to unintentionally and inevitably annoying her in-laws.

It was amusing to be on the video call, throughout her moving process. Watching her panic, as the movers tried to fit her antique wardrobe through his bedroom door, was especially entertaining. Her ex was already willing to sacrifice his door to keep her wardrobe intact.

"Get me my tools! I'll take down this door by myself!" he had yelled as Sophie panicked over her wardrobe being "too big" to fit through the door. The movers then suggested something "barbaric", according to Sophie. But, eventually, they did end up dismantling and rebuilding her precious vintage wardrobe inside her new bedroom.

According to Sophie, the doors do not swing open as smoothly as they used to. And, I will take her side if it ever becomes a bigger argument.

She keeps calling me from time to time. And I hope I can visit her, soon. It may have just been a week but, it seems like time is flying away and we might never meet again, at least not like we used to.

Wine and cheesy popcorn, keep reminding me of her, every time I walk into Jay's pantry. They just stand out in between boxes of oats, ground millet and other nutrition-rich ingredients. And I wonder if he asked Sophie about what snacks I like, before he restocked his super-healthy pantry.

Did he really do all that, just for me?

Maybe I'll ask her about it when we meet. Or, maybe, I'll just continue living in my delusional bubble and keep believing that Jay makes affectionate efforts for me and wants me to be a part of more than just his business. A little imagination never hurt anyone, right?

Speaking of business, the cafe has managed to survive a week without me. And, as usual, Sophie was right! I should focus on the creative side of the business and let our staff run the place. After all, Jay is also around to keep an eye on everything.

This forced and unplanned staycation has helped me focus on my creative priorities. And the beautiful skies have been inspirational. I've come up with more new ideas over the past week than I did in the past couple of months.

Jay managed to bake some of my new ideas for a whole range of breakfast treats. We thinks we can turn it into a whole new concept for customers who are always running late and can only managed to grab a coffee on-the-go. Some of them have potential and we plan on giving out a few trial batches at the cafe over the next few days.

Everything seems normal until I think about the lunatic trying to hurt us and my business partner having to harbor me. It's mortifying at time, like that one night when I bumped into his soap lathered chest.

He had rushed out of his bedroom, wrapped in equal parts of fluffy towel and soapy bubbles. He said he had to check if the pie was burning in the oven. And I tried my best not to focus on how the soapy water slid down his sculpted chest.

As he walked back to his bedroom, it amused me to know that his back looked even better in person than it did on that slightly distorted parking lot mirror. And I almost did not slip and fall on the small puddle of soapy water that he left behind on the kitchen floor.

Almost!

As time passed, we slowly found a way to not let awkward moments bother us. Sharing a chore-chart made things easier and more efficient. And, before I knew it, I started organizing color-coded sticky notes on his refrigerator.

It is my turn to cook on the seventh morning of waking up in a house that isn't my home. But, I've slowly gotten used to finding my way around Jay's kitchen. We have even managed to synchronize our movements to avoid bumping into each other as we prepare any meal, together. Somehow, all the time we spend in the cafe, makes it easier to find a rhythm going inside any kitchen. But, it still feels different from when we are working together.

Is this getting a little too domestic?

It feels domestic.

"I think I found out where the twins are at!" Jay informs me while we have breakfast.

He takes a sip of his coffee before he adds "I'm heading over there with my detective friend. I was planning on going on my own but he clearly loves working too much, even on his day off."

Jay chuckles and, I want to say that he does the same thing. But, who am I to lecture him about overworking? I stayed up late, three nights in a row, working on a range of new vegan options for our customers.

"That's great news! Do you want me to come with you?" I ask, hoping to get some fresh air. And, by fresh, I mean the usual city air that smells like gasoline and smoke. I miss the not-so-breezy city air.

"It might be better if you stay. I've given all the necessary instructions to Sarah. And the new bakery intern seems to be helpful. They can manage on their own. But, it would be better if you are available, in case they need any help. Plus, those two women haven't been seen at the cafe, ever since that man showed up. Someone needs to talk to them, if and when they do show up again." he insists that it's the best option for us. But, I think he is continuously worried.

If I wasn't happy, right now, I'd probably think that he does not want me to leave this house, ever again! But, I'm learning to trust his instincts, and my own.

"Hey! I promise I'll be back, soon. And I'll make sure we find something important. I'll not let that man hurt any of us again." Jay gentle rubs the back of my palm before retreating his hand.

Should I ask him to hold my hand for a little while longer, before he leaves?

"Alright!" I keep my thoughts to myself, for now.

The detective arrives and Jay leaves with a few pairs of clothes and a big full of refreshments. I guess he will be away for a few days. And the house starts feeling empty again.

I try to keep myself busy but there is only so much one can do on their own. Thankfully, someone from the cafe calls and suggests that I urgently come over. It wasn't a voice that I recognized at first but it was probably Sarah. Or at least, I hope it was.

A town cab gets me to the cafe in a little less than an hour. And, as I'm entering through the door, for the first time in a week, I see two familiar faces on one of the corner tables, inside the cafe.

It's them!

I quickly walk over to Sarah and ask if they have been around for a while.

"They are having their third cup of coffee and I'm making their fourth. Maybe you should take it to them and see if you can stir up a conversation?" she suggests and I agree. It's now or never.

"Hello Ladies! Enjoying the sunny Sunday?" I ask while setting down their order on the table.

"It's you, isn't it?" one of them asks me before adding "You're the one he was looking for, right?".

"He?" I act oblivious.

"We know you're looking for him and we also know he has been lurking around this cafe. Do you know him? Are you helping him?" she furrows her brows.

"Helping him? He attacked my best friend! I haven't been able to go home in a week. I am not helping him. I am hiding from him, just like you are!" I snap and instantly regret my outburst.

But the other woman, who looks a bit older, suggests "We can talk somewhere else. Our apartment is not too far from here!".

And what am I supposed to do? Go alone? Say no? Make another scene by getting mad at them, again?

So, I decide to ask "Would you mind if I bring someone along with me?".

"Sure!" says the older woman while the younger one keeps grinding her teeth at me.

She's scary.

Sarah and I, soon find ourselves in their apartment, looking around for an escape plan, even before they can close the front door.

"Sit!" the older woman says and we slump down on the couch in their living room. It's comfy, until I worry about their possible intentions.

The younger woman grabs a chair from across the room while looking for something on her phone. She places the chair in front of us and takes a seat as she says "A detective has been roaming around and trying to find information about my ex husband!".

She turns her phone towards us and adds "This man is capable of a lot more than you can imagine!".

The pictures of the man, the one who attacked Sophie, seems oddly normal. Without any rage on his face, it seems like just another picture of just another man who is busy living his mundane life. He looks like a decent husband and a decent father from just that one picture. And I worry how he might have seemed normal to so many people in his life, until he showed his true colors.

"I think it's clear that he isn't exactly normal. But how much is he really capable of?" I ask and she replies "He used to be a man capable of loving and living a normal life. But now, he is just breathing to seek revenge. And that pretty little business partner boyfriend of yours..." she pauses and grinds her teeth again.

"Not my boyfriend!" I protest without certainty. I'm not exactly sure who Jay is, beyond my business partner and a man who insists of being a knight in shining armor, whether we need one or not.

"Whatever!" she sounds angry. "That pretty boy has been lying to you. You are not the reason why my ex is stalking you or hurting people you love. He is!

"How?" I question, sternly. Because, it's usually something I did. It's usual someone who I offend just by having an opinion or just simply existing. I know that Jay has some connection with the twins. But what more could there be?

As I'm trying to wrap my head around the possibilities, the older woman replies "Your business partner's father is my husband's half brother. And my husband isn't after you or your cafe or your best friend because you did something wrong. He is after everything that is dear to your business partner, and I guess that it includes you!".

Sarah gasps and covers her face. I can see her holding in a scream. But she probably thinks this is dramatic rather than dangerous. Why else would she tag along when she knows the risks? Maybe she thinks that this is some mystery adventure and not someone's actually life spinning out of control.

"Sarah! Go call the detective and ask him to bring Jay back home. And tell him that it's urgent. Tell him that we found out something important about the case." I instruct Sarah who instantly excuses herself from the conversation and makes the call.

"He wants to talk to you!" she tries handing me the phone but I shake my head. So she continues talking to the detective.

"Yeah! Yeah! She's busy! Yeah! Okay! Yes! I'll be sure to tell her that! Yes! Okay!" she mumbles before hanging up.

"What did the detective say?"

"He said that Jay suddenly left and he can't trace the twins either. He is on his way back and he wants you to go back to your own apartment. There's a squad car waiting for you there. They will be on call, in case you need any help." Sarah looks excited!

Why are all these youngster so excited about real-life drama? It's not like there is a rewind button in life! What if someone stabs or shoots me?

"Fine! Go back to the cafe. And don't tell anyone about any of this until I'm back, okay?" I instruct her and she promptly agrees to follow the order. But I highly doubt that she will not be gossiping, at least a little bit, at least about Jay.

But where is Jay? And where are the twins?

"Do you happen to know where your twins might be?" I ask and the older woman squints at me as she escorts Sarah to the door.

Once door has closed between Sarah and the rest of us, she replies "Listen to me, very carefully! You can not trust anyone, including the twins. They left home last year and we think that they may have been helping their father.".

Her gaze shifts towards the younger woman who is gently holding her hand and patting her back. And it reminds of just how badly I miss having someone to count on. It reminds me that Sophie and I might never meet as often as we used to and Sophie might not need me like she used to.

I miss her.

The younger women continue the conversation with, what looks like deep regret in her eyes.

"The kids have had to go thought a lot. And I should never have taken my ex's money for the separation settlement. It was my fault that he ended up being broke and took it out on them. I've been trying to make amends, even since I found out about their situation. That's is why I offered them my home, this home. But, now that the kids aren't even here anymore, everything feels empty without their cheers and chatter."

She pauses to look around, just for a few seconds. And my eyes follow her gaze. The apartment looks beautiful, considering it's age. And it does not seem like they have made too many changes to it's vintage decor. It reminds me of a part of our family home that was lost to bad restoration.

I look at her and wait for some potentially useful information. But I also what to know if she has a family of her own, if she is still in touch with them, and if they forgive her for the mistakes of her youth.

"I...I wish I never met him." she sobs. And I wonder if that's the kind of people we are; people who get hurt and blame ourselves about everything that happens in our troubled past.

I can see the older woman furrow her brows and say "It was not your fault. I should have left him after discovering how he cheated on me. The kids deserved better than a dysfunctional family that keep holding on for the sake of traditions.".

As I watch them blaming themselves for the actions of an unstable man, I wonder how the twins must be feeling right now. I wonder if they eat properly or they skip meals, like I did, when I first started living on my own. I wonder how the twins are making money to pay for their survival. And I wonder if Jay knows about any of this. He must know! He always seems to know a lot. And if he does, why hasn't he told me about it?

"How do we stop him? And how do we get your twins back home?" I asks and she replies "We don't have to find the twins. They know their way back home. They are old enough and strong enough. It's their choice now. I will not take any more decisions for them. I'll just wait for them to forgive us.".

I can hear the hurt in her voice and see the hope in her eyes. And I wonder if that's how my family feels about me. I hope they look forward to having me back home, someday.

"And we don't stop my husband!" she adds. "We let him think that he can do whatever he wants. Eventually, he will get overconfident and sloppy. And that's the only chance we will have to run, as far away from him as we can.".

"But why should we run? We did nothing wrong. It's our lives, our homes, our dreams. And we worked hard for it. Shouldn't we fight for what's ours?"

"Isn't he doing the same thing? Fight for something that used to be his? Seeking safety is not a weakness, even if we have to run for it." she frowns and I sigh, finding it hard to disagree.

"Moreover, it isn't our fight anymore!" she adds while straightening her brows.

"So, who's is it? Jay's?" I ask and she nods.

"Talk to him!" she insisted. "Only he can make amends. You can not beat my husband with rage. You must kill his rage with your kindness.".

After I leave their apartment, I decide to walk back to my home. It's just a couple of blocks away. But, the skies are weighing down on the bustling city. There are dark clouds that rumble and startle some of the pedestrians. And I think about the raincoat that I threw into a trashcan, just a week ago.

As I take a turn from the intersection, I can see the squad car that is parked in front of my building. The plates are familiar. But, it seems to be a new team.

I wave at the officers and they wave back before one of them steps out of the car. A raindrop splatters on the windshield of the squad car, just as the officer walks up to me.

"Glad you're here before the storm hits! Try not to wander around, until we catch that guy. And call us if you need our help!" the officers hands me a card with her number inked and embossed on it. And I nod before thanking her and heading up to my apartment.

It feels weird. Being home, after such a long time, feels incomplete. And, I wonder if I miss Jay's place or Jay himself.

Now that everyone doubts him and his motives, why am I leaning towards trusting him and his instincts?

Today's mood went from happiness to confusion to worry and anxiety. And, I don't think I can sleep tonight.

The rain starts slow. Small droplets settle on my windows before they accumulate and buckle under their own weight. The rainwater sliding down the glass, look like tears running down my cheeks. And, before I can even realize, the thundering skies are masking the sounds of my sorrow.

• *Diary Entry* •

Bullying has the power to scar your soul. It's not just a physical wound that can heal over time. It distorts the way you experience the world around you. Anything can scare, annoy or trigger you, in ways that you can least expect or predict.

On a slow and seemingly insignificant evening, I bumped into a women who looked just like her. She did look a few years older. But, that was natural. What happened in college, was a long time ago.

I thought that it was just another coincidence. I tried to convince myself that I keep seeing her in every women I came across. But, my gut knew that it was definitely her.

It was a surprisingly relaxed evening. The captain had offered to pay for our drinks and the squad was excited. We were occupying the large booth near the bar counter. She was sitting next to us, on a two topper table that was closest to the exit.

There was nothing but a bottle of beer keeping her company. Her fingers tapped on the glass bottle as her wandering gaze scanned her surroundings. I was not sure if she wanted to be left alone or she was waiting for someone to show up. But, after a while, I assumed that she was on her own.

So, I thought that we should turn around and say hello, and maybe give her some company. But, a random man came over and asked if any of us had a lighter. The bartender asked him to use the smoking room while handing him a matchbox. Beer soaked fingers pointing towards a small glass booth towards the back of the bar. But, the man lit his cigarette, right there, right next to us.

It was infuriating. I wanted to drag him out of the bar and put him into the squad car. He definitely deserved to spend a night in the slammer. But, instead of doing that, I was drawn towards the sudden change in her demeanor.

Her shoulders had stiffened and I could see the discomfort in her eyes. And, maybe that was life's way of signaling the alarm to wake me up. Maybe it was life's way of telling me that it was my chance to recognize her and beg for forgiveness. But, it took me a little too long to react.

The next thing I know, she was throwing her beer bottle at the man, pushing her table aside and running away. It took me a moment to process what had just happened, and I quickly ran behind her. I tried catching up, I really did. But, she swiftly got into a cab that promptly drove her away.

When I got back into the bar, one of our officers had already apprehended the smoker for attacking the bartender with a half-smashed beer bottle. In that moment, I had no idea how things had escalated so quickly. The bartender was hyperventilating from behind the counter, patrons were being instructed to leave, and I could hear an ambulance pulling over, right outside the main entrance of the bar.

It was such a strange sequence of events for a seemingly slow evening. And, I kept wondering why rage was such a destructive emotion.

That's when I knew that I had to find her, at any cost. I had to find her and make amends. She could finally start healing, if I apologized to her. And I could finally sleep without nightmares, if she forgave me.

I desperately hoped that she would forgive me, and I desperately hoped that I would deserve it.

CHAPTER 7

A LONG DRIVE DOWN MEMORY LANE
(From the point of view of the Detective)

The sun keeps playing hide and seek as I drive out of the city. A cloud that look like a handful of fluff cotton balls, seem to be following me with every turn of the wheels. The unusually heavy traffic, choked almost every exit. But, I barely made it out of the city limits before noon.

As I pull into Jay's driveway, the radio starts playing an old song from almost a decade ago. I'm not even sure how I ended up on this frequency but, fate has always enjoyed playing mind games with me.

"Hey! Sorry I'm late! Let's go!" Jay announces as he opens the door and let's himself into my car.

"Gently, please!" I ask Jay, not to bang the door close because, I'm driving my personal vehicle for the trip. Taking the squad car to meet the twins can't possibly be helpful. Plus, the captain will want to know why I need the squad car on my day off.

"Are we going there to find the twins or are you planning on moving there?" I ask as I watch him shove his big bag into the back seat. And I truly wonder why he is always prepared for an end-of-the-world kind of scenario.

"I thought we were not going to stop on the way there. So I just brought some snacks, and some change of clothes." he replies, casually.

As I'm driving northwards and we leave the state limits, Jay slowly goes silent. He is usually talkative but, right now, he is focusing on his phone screen.

"What's with you?"

"Huh?" he mumbles and keeps typing.

"I've never seen you stay quite for such a long time! Is everything okay?"

"Yeah! Just texting something important to the cafe staff."

"Hmmm!" I'm not convinced. But I'm not here to interrogate him. I'm just here to find the twins and hopefully catch the person who attacked Ms. Park-View Penthouse, and vandalized that one table in Jay's pretentious cafe.

Seriously, who even pays twelve bucks for a doughnut?

"Hey! Why exactly are you getting involved in all this? Don't to have those suited up people who deal with everything?" I finally question him. But he replies with another question.

"Do you remember what had happened to the twins, before they moved away?"

"Hmmm! Of course. But that was ages ago. How is that connected to any of this?"

"Do you still think about it?"

"I try not to think about the past." I tightly grip the steering wheel. This is making me uncomfortable. Why are we talking about the past?

"Do you regret what happened after that day?"

"Of course!" I sigh. This is exhausting. Why is he trying to bring the past into all this?

"Do you ever wish that we did something differently, back then?" he asks while turning his head towards me. His eyes are burning into the side of my face. And it feels hot, so hot.

"All the time! I wish I was a better person. I wish I did the right thing." I respond but I wish we were not having this conversation right now.

"And you know what, Jay? That was not the only time I did not help someone who needed my help. I was a coward. But I have changed. I have dedicated my entire career for helping people in need. Why? Because I still feel guilty about everything that happened in the past. I try to help people because I could not find the courage when my family name was weighing me down! But my job gives me the power to stand tall and to do the right thing."

Jay looks at me for a while, with an unfamiliar expression. Is it pity in his eyes or just sincere sympathy? I wonder why he seems different today.

"I know!" he pauses for a second before going on. "Everyone just turned a blind eye to any such incident back then.

Bullying was normal. Everyone was being mocked and harassed by someone. At least you always tried your best! I know you tried helping the twins back then."

"Tried! But I was not able to! They deserved better! I wonder if things would have been different if I actually had their back!" I grip the steering wheel tighter and tighter. This is reminding me of things from the past that I do not want to think about.

"You were just a kid." Jay reminds me. "We all were. And you did enough! They beat you up and you still tried your best to protect the twins for that obnoxious brat." he sounds a little annoyed as he recalls the day. And I try to believe him. But it's hard.

Was I helpful? Was it enough? I wonder why everyone else stayed silent about what was going on. Wasn't it everyone's fault? If we had stopped that bully back then, would he have been able to hurt those women in college? And, wasn't it my fault that I did not report him after that basement incident? Was I ever helpful to anyone while growing up? Or did I just worry about my family name and our reputation? My head hurts from all the questions that keep reminding me that I have never done enough and I'll never be forgiven.

"Look!" Jay turns the radio off and continues. "I'm getting involved in all this because the twins deserved better than my silence. They have been through enough. And I truly think that they can help us, if we help them too. Maybe, this way, we can finally make amends."

While I'm not fully convinced that the twins will be helpful, I do think he is right. We have to make amends. It is long overdue.

"You're right! But shouldn't you keep your distance and be a little careful? Who knows what the twins have been up to. What if they still hold a grudge?"

"Being careful about what happens to us, is the reason we are all in this mess right now!" he sighs. He seems distant these days. Is it just stress from the recent incidents? Or is it something more?

"You tell me not to blame myself, not to be hard on myself. But I think you still blame yourself for what happened after that day when the twins finally left."

Jay doesn't reply.

The silence keeps us company until we reach the infamous "clown" town and I drive into the territory of Sheriff Know-It-All. He warned me never to bring my random investigations into his town after that one "missing person case" turned out to be a mass kidnapping fiasco. But, I'm not exactly here for an investigation, per say. I'm just here to find some good old friends from school.

"Hey! Do you need some coffee?" I ask Jay. He has been way too quite for far too long. He even hung up on some calls about half an hour ago. Something does not seem right.

"How much longer until we reach?" he asks.

"Another hour, I guess. Maybe an hour and a half, if there's traffic."

"It might get dark, by the time we get there. The weather is far too gloomy today. Maybe we should get a room for the night? We can meet the twin in the morning!" he suggests.

"Listen! We are not on a road trip right now!" I laugh. But honestly, I miss those days when we did not have any responsibility and road trips were a last-minute cure for heartaches. Is that why we have been friends for so long? Having dealt with a lot of heartaches, together?

"What if the twins hesitate to meet us?" he asks with a serious pout. It's been a while since I've seen him make the face.

"Then we will just have to make something up, so they do not ditch the meeting!"

"And what if it gets too late or it rains too hard and we can't find a place to stay?" he whines.

"We will cross that bridge when we get there. For now, let's focus on pinpointing their location and convincing them to meet us, in public." I suggest because, I truly do not trust the twins. I think they are up to something. And I think Jay knows about it.

"All this is making me feel sick. I think I need a cup of coffee. Can we please stop somewhere?" he asks while rolling down the window. He seems anxious. Is this situation triggering him again?

"Thought you brought your entire kitchen along with you!" I joke, of course. But he doesn't respond. He usually laughs at my jokes, even if he isn't feeling great. He used to say that my jokes heal him.

I wonder if he is okay.

"Look! There's a diner ahead. Let's get you a cup of coffee, or maybe a lemonade? And I'll have what you're having, just like old times!"

I pull over and Jay springs out of his side, leaning the door open as he walks a few steps away from where we are parked.

Is he hyperventilating?

I grab a paper bag from my glove compartment and rush out of the car. His shoulders are tense and his breathing is hurried. It was not a good idea for him to get involved in all this.

"Here! Take this!" I try to hand him the bag.

But he pushes it away and says "I'm fine! I'm fine!".

"You don't look fine!" I say while closing the car door and pocketing my keys.

"I will be, when I get some coffee." he insists as he rushes into the diner and frantically throws his hands around, asking for a cup of coffee. And I stand a few feet away from him and his flailing arms.

The women behind the counter, grabs the pot with decaf written on it's handle. She must be used to dealing hyperventilating customers more often than I would have guessed.

"Same for you?" she asks me and I nod.

We grab a seat by the window and she sets our coffee cups down, points at the menu on the board and walks away.

When Jay seems to have finally calmed down, after chugging most of his lukewarm coffee, I decide to continue the conversation.

"Look! You did enough back then. You were just a kid. It was not your responsibility to protect other children in the school. You were friendly and kind. That was a lot better than what anyone else did in that school. And that incident was not our fault. But yes, we should definitely make amends, any way we can, without hurting ourselves. You look like you are about to pop a vein on your forehead. Let's do this, one step at a time, okay? And let's start with finding the twins!"

Jay swirls the leftover coffee in his cup as he says "I have unfinished business. Taking it one step at a time is pointless now. I have to fix things before anyone else gets hurt!".

I wonder if this whole case is more than just the vandalism or the attack or even the twins. Why is he taking it so personally, after such a long time? Is any of this even about helping the twins?

"Hey! Let's head back on the road huh? We still have an hour long drive until we get to that place where the twins were supposedly working at. So, maybe they live nearby?" I suggest as I get off my seat.

"Wait! Let me pay!" Jay announces, as usual.

"No! Stay! I'll pay! Be right back!" I insist.

"Fine! I'll just use the restroom real quick!" he says, while walking towards the back of the diner.

"Alright! I'll wait in the car!"

I pay the bill as I ask the woman behind the counter if she has ever seen the twins around. She looks at the picture and looks at me for a few seconds before saying that she has never seen them before.

Worth a shot!

I think about her pause, as I walk back to my car. Jay should not take too long. So I turn on the radio again while I wait. But one song becomes two and Jay has not returned yet.

I walk back into the diner and check the washroom. But, Jay is nowhere to be found.

"Is there a back door around here?" I ask a man who is exiting from the washroom. He is dressed like the woman behind the counter. So I assume that he must have been working here for a while. Their pants are the same shade of navy blue that looks overused. His shirt is the same shade of pale yellow as the woman's apron. And I wonder if it was white, when it was first made.

"There is a service door. But no one is allowed back there!" the man rushes back to the cash register while replying to me.

Did he even wash his hands?

I run out of the front door and rush to the back of the diner. And, while there is no one there, I do find an old road, leading eastwards from the route we have been on.

"Where did you go, Jay? Don't make me send out men to look for you, too!" I grind my teeth as I make some calls. This is exhausting. I just wanted to help my friends.

"Hey mister!" The woman from the diner, yells at me and asks me to move my car.

"You're blocking the entrance." she screams as I walk past her and get back into my car.

And, as I start driving towards the last known location of the twins, the captain calls and suggests that I get back to the city. He asks me to find out another way to track the attacker.

No amount of protest is enough to convince him, especially after he informs me about an anonymous tip that came in, early today. It mentioned a possible location of the attacker and asked the PD to send a specific detective; me. It's strange but I have no chance to ask why or how the anonymous tip came in, just for me. The captain sounds furious and he reminds me that we need to close this case, as fast as possible.

The call disconnects before I can protest any further. And it's frustrating. I wondering what Jay is up to, right now. What is he trying to hide from me? What is his unfinished business with the twins?

I keep wondering, as I hear a buzzing sound. The vibrations are coming from the passenger seat. Eventually, I realize that it must be my phone and I might have tossed it away, after the captain ordered me to get back to the city.

Since when have I become so hot headed?

When I pull over and check the number, I notice that it's a call from Sarah, a barista from Jay's cafe. She was supposed to call me, if and when something went wrong. There is no other reason for her to contact me. So, I worry, wondering if someone got hurt, again.

This is exhausting!

I just wanted to help Jay, and Sophie, and most importantly, his business partner. I was doing this for her. I just wanted to make amends.

This seemed like the best opportunity and it was in my wheelhouse. And I should have been able to solve this case, by now. But, in hindsight, this was probably not the best way to make amends.

I must ask for her forgiveness, without letting this case and these worries engulf my entire existence.

I need to find a better way to make things right. And, I need a new diary. It's important that I process my feelings that are separate from our shared history.

CHAPTER 8

JAY, KAY, ELL AND ZED
(From the point of view of Jay)

"Is everything ready?" I text from the restroom. And the response comes almost instantaneous.

"Back door! Black sedan with 777 plate. Kay will drive you there and she has already acquired your essentials. Be quick!"

I hand in a generous tip to the diner staff, who opens the back door for me. And I quickly slip into the car.

"Where's, Zed?" I ask and Kay replies "He's tracking down the man as we speak.".

"Does dad know about any of this?"

"No, sir! He is under the impression that you are on a business trip!"

A business trip for the cafe owner, the family disappointment, the failed heir?

"You convinced him with a lie like that?" I ask while looking out of the window. These roads have become far too familiar by now. But this is the first time I am not driving down this route on my own.

"He thinks that you are acquiring a few units outside the country. We asked your usual realtor to vouch for you."

"How much?"

"Excuse me?" Kay questions while taking a turn. Where did she learn how to drive so smoothly? Did my brother teach her the tricks that he taught me? Maybe he taught her a lot more that just driving like a pro. Maybe I could have learned a lot more, if I gave the family business a chance.

"How much did you pay my realtor?" I asks while scrolling through my phone and checking my bank account balance. But it's unchanged. Did my brother pay for it? This is frustrating because, how am I supposed to pay him back? He always refuses to let me help him with anything.

"It's been handled, sir. Your realtor friend will no longer bill you for little favors like this."

It's funny. My friends think that I'm the scary one. In reality, my brother and his people are far scarier than I can ever be. Even I don't know what "handled" truly means. Maybe I should pay my realtor a visit, after all this is settled.

I bring my attention back to my phone again and dial a number that I have memorized by now. When the call connects, the ringing chimes in my ear and amps up my anxiety, until someone picks up.

"Who's this?" a familiar voice asks, harshly, from the other side of the call.

"It's me! Did you get the delivery from Zed?

"Hmmm. Last night."

"I'm on my way!"

"Are you finally alone?"

"It's just me, and Kay!"

"Airtight! You know where to find us!"

I hang up and ask Kay to turn off the navigation system. I can guide her from here. We are almost there. Just another mile and a half.

And when we finally pull over, a ask Kay to stay in the car and not entertain any call, not even my own.

"Yes, sir!" she replies before I step out. The doors lock and the windows roll up as I step away from the car and walk towards the motel.

Room number 304! The twins have been staying there since I first found them. They had found my number, somehow, and called me after being kicked out of their rental. And what was I supposed to do? Ignore them? They needed someone to help them. And I was more than capable of doing the bare essentials.

knock knock knock

I wait for a few seconds until I see the door handle turning and the wooden barricade slowly making way.

"Did anyone follow you?" he asks and I shake my head. But he still checks the corridor before letting me in.

As I take a seat, the twins offer me water and a snack. The room looks dark with the curtains drawn closer. The dim bulb is not enough to light the entire room. Their beds look overused. Do they ever leave their room? This is heartbreaking.

"Did Zed get you everything you needed?" I ask and they nods.

"Let me know if you need anything else, okay? Zed should be back in a couple of days."

"Hmmm. That's fine but, when can we go back home?" he asks.

"Soon!"

"You have been saying that for a while now!" he sounds a little annoyed. Understandable, but also a little scary.

"Give me a week! One week!"

He laughs and it feels so dark. The sound of distrust, echoes inside your ears, like a bitter taste that lingers on your tongue for days. It sticks to your soul and engulfs the last rays of hope with darkness.

"Where is he now?" she asks while he grinds his teeth next to me. I can also see him balling his fists. Maybe I shouldn't have asked Kay to not entertain any calls, not even my own.

I know they are not capable of violence. But I'm a little worried about his mood right now.

Who could blame him? They have been forced to stay away from home and put their lives on hold. Maybe I shouldn't have waited for so long to find a solution. Maybe I should have asked my brother to help us, back when I first reconnect with the twins.

"Zed is looking for him. We have found out where he lives!" I reply before taking a sip of the water.

"What then? What happens when you find him?" he asks with his piercing gaze pinning me in place.

No wonder everyone thinks that they might be dangerous. They have been through so much. The rage is boiling in his eyes. Who knows how much time remains, until the rage breaks through.

"We go ahead with the plan. And I promise you, I will get you two back home soon. One week, please! Just wait for another week." I try to sound sincere but honestly, I'm not sure how long it may take. That is why I asked my brother to get involved.

I'm trying! Our people are trying. But how long can I expect the twins to wait. They need to get their life back. They deserve better than this dingy motel room and half-baked promises.

"Fine! We will wait. But please send Zed as soon as you can. We might need some help before we move back home. You're not the only one with unfinished business." he sounds calmed and scarier at the same time. And I wonder if it's just me or does calmness truly feel more unsettling than chaos.

"Do you want me to stay here for the night?" I ask but they suggest I should stay somewhere else.

"You think I can't handle a motel room?" I chuckle.

"Yes! We know you can't handle these beds!" he laughs at me. But honestly, that's better than him punching me.

"I'm sorry it took me so long to help you guys!" I apologize. I always do. They think it's unnecessary but I think I need to apologize, until I help them get their life back.

"Go on! Get out of here. Kay will freak out if you stay out of her sight for too long. I don't want her to threaten me again. She's scary." he laughs again.

Maybe we are all scared and easily rattled. Maybe it's because we have all been holding our guard up, for so long, that it scares us to let it down, even for a second. Maybe we have lived in fear for so long that even the bare minimum makes us worry.

I wish someone could have helped them sooner.

We say our goodbyes and I promise them to have this matter resolved, once and for all. They don't seem convinced and I try not to verbally assure them, over and over again.

I'm done talking. Now is the time to act!

When I get back to the car, Kay is on a video call with my brother. She hangs up and panics for a second, before she opens the door for me.

Everyone has something to fear, something to hide. And yet, we all act tough and invincible.

"What did he say?" I ask her as she drive us out of the motel parking lot.

"Excuse me?"

"My brother! What did he say, before you hung up?"

"He was just asking if we reached safely."

"My brother? He asked you that? Are you really such a good liar? I almost want to believe you."

"He cares for you, sir! It is not unusual for him to make sure that you are alright!"

She sounds sincere but I'm not sure if I trust that anyone in my family cares about me. Maybe they just don't want me to be the reason for another embarrassment.

"Did Zed call?"

"He did! He found the man and they are on their way to..." she pauses when her phone starts ringing.

"It's for you, sir!" she passes me her phone.

I check the number of the display and it's Zed!

"Did you take care of everything?" I ask and Zed replies "Yes, sir! It's done. He wouldn't be a problem anymore. I've also asked Ell to make sure that it stays under the radar.".

Now who the heck is Ell? How many people are even working for my little brother? Isn't he a little too young to know how to handle such difficult situations so well? How much pocket money is dad paying him? Or is it his own money, from that fancy side gig of his?

He is born to fit the family name! He can protect the family business, better than I ever could. I'm better off in my cafe.

Thank God, my parents have him. I could never live up to their expectations, the way my little brother does.

I'm so proud of him! Maybe I should say that to him, someday. It's been a while since we last met.

CHAPTER 9

HOME SWEET HOME

It's been a month since Jay left. I've settled back into my apartment but, sleeping alone is still a struggle. The cafe is doing well and it's keeping me busy throughout the day. But, I keep missing him.

Do I miss seeing him at work? Do I miss having him around? I'm not sure why exactly I miss him but, I know that I do.

Earlier this month, woman named Kay had delivered a notebook for the cafe staff. It had all of Jay's meticulous measurements, noted down in his beautiful handwriting. She insisted that the new bakery intern was capable of handling it and Jay had already taught him most of the recipes. I was not convinced, until the intern managed to replicate many of the recipes that only Jay had mastered.

Maybe we should hire him as a full time employee. I can't possibly do all the work on my own, in case Jay decides not to come back.

I wonder why Jay left so unceremoniously. He does not reply to my texts anymore. Sophie and I tried calling him throughout the first couple of weeks since he went away. But he kept disconnecting our calls until he eventually turned off his phone.

I wonder what happened to him.

Those two women have been coming to the cafe on Sundays. They keep insisting that I visit them, again. But, what am I supposed to do? Small talk is not my thing and they do not seem to be chatty. And, I've been politely declining their invitation, until today.

The cafe is closed for the weekend, for scheduled maintenance. Our regulars have been informed about it in advance. The staff have been sent away for a long weekend off, except for the intern, who insisted on handling the pre-orders from a satellite kitchen. I tried helping but he sent me back home, earlier this morning.

My day is completely free and I do not feel like staying home alone for any longer than I need to. So, I grab a bottle of wine and a bunch of flowers as I head towards their apartment. It's a quick walk as the roads are not as busy as usual. The pedestrian lanes are not nearly as crowded and I quickly walk past the intersection until I reach their building.

The elevator is old but it looks gorgeous. I did not notice it, the last time I was here. The place looks like a movie set or a slice of history. Rent must be expensive. And, for someone who has been on the run with a virtual stranger and two kids, these women definitely live in a posh neighborhood.

I wonder how they managed to afford this place.

When I finally reach their apartment, the women seem cheerful, even youthful, somehow. I'm not sure what changed but it's nice to see their smiles.

As I walk down the hallway that leads to their living room, I notice their refrigerator and the magnets on them. They remind me of my brother and make me wonder if either of them have a sibling, like I do. And I wonder if their families miss them, or have tried to forgot about them, after years of being apart. I even wonder if they ever tried meeting their families, after they moved here. Because, it must be so hard to live away from your loved ones for such a long time.

"Thanks for coming!" they say as they gently nudge me towards the couch, until I take a seat. The younger woman accepts the flowers with a smile, and the older woman thanks me for the wine.

I still feel awkward for not remembering their real names till date. And it's just too embarrassing to ask them about it again, after such a long time. But they seem to remember mine. So, I worry if that makes me a bad person for not remembering people's names, even when I try to remember everything else.

"Thanks for inviting me. How have you been? Did you hear from the twins?" I ask as they bring me a glass of milk and a box full of assorted cookies.

The box looks adorable and I make a mental note to try some new packaging designs for our pre-orders and brunch bookings.

As I wait for their response, their smiles brighten. It's comforting. My heart flutters with hope. It's too early in the day to have hope make my heart skip a beat. But, I let myself feel the warmth of hope.

"We have a surprise for you!" the women say as they rush into another room and drag two people out into the living room.

"They are home! They finally came home!" their mother sounds ecstatic.

"We finally meet!" I say, awkwardly, not knowing how else to greet people I don't fully recognize. I had only ever seen the twins in pictures, from over a year ago. They look different in person. The girl is taller than I thought she would be and the boy looks older.

"It's their birthday, next week! Our babies are back home before their birthday!" their mother says while stroking their hair. The joy on her face is only rivaled by the one on their own. I've never imagined the twins looking so gentle. Their smiles truly fill life into the old and exhausted walls around us.

"You should come! We can all celebrate, together!" the younger woman suggests and I nod.

Together!

I wonder where Jay might be, right now.

"How did the two of you get back home?" I ask, hoping for it to somehow be connected to Jay.

"Jay helped us. Do you know Zed? He brought us back home. Jay helped us get away from that stalker psychopath." the boy's smile fades, just enough to show his resentment.

"Hey! Don't say that. He is still your father!" his mother scolds him. "And he is getting the help he needs. He will get better. I'm sure he will. You have to trust Jay. He said he will help us."

As she tries to reason with her son, I try to make sense of why Jay keep running around, helping everyone he can. It's confusing to think of the possible reasons why he feel obligated to get involved in everyone else's chaos. And, I resent him, a little, for leaving me behind.

I'm mad at him. I know that he owes me no explanation. But, my heart thinks that he should have told me why he left. My heart foolishly wants to believe that I deserve an explanation for being abandoned when I was just starting to get comfortable in his presence.

"How's Jay? Did you meet him after coming back home?" I ask the twins.

"No! But we did meet him just before Zed drove us back home. He looked tired. But he enthusiastically talked about you. Are you dating him or something?" the girl asks with a mischievous smile. "I've never seen him talk about anyone, so fondly. In fact, he had never talked about his personal life before he mentioned you."

I'm confused. He can talk about me but not with me? Now I'm really mad at him.

"What did he say?" I ask with a frown and the girl continues "He said that he needs to fix this before he can go back home to someone he adores. He said something about a couch but I'm not sure what he meant by that. He kept mumbling about the couch before looking embarrassed and asking us to leave. And then Zed drove us back home.".

Why is Jay such a menace? Can't he just come back home already? I miss him. I want to punch him and ask him why he thought that it was a good idea to hide everything from me, including his feelings.

"Didn't Jay call you, after he got back home?" the boy asks me. And I shake my head before I reply "I had no idea that he was back!".

I try not to sound bitter. Because, I'm getting tired of being mad at someone who isn't mine, until he says so, out loud. But, I'm disappointed at myself for letting my expectations hurt me.

"We have known Jay since Middle School. And we both know that he cares for you, in a way that he hasn't cared for others. And we are sure that he will reach out, soon!" the boy smiles, reassuringly.

"Thanks for saying that. I'll keep it in mind while I get mad at him." I chuckle to lighten the mood. And the twins grin, mischievously.

"Is there anything else that you may be hiding from me?" I ask and they aggressively shake their heads.

They are adorable. So young and so full of life.

OH!

They are so young. Did they say that they studied with Jay? Is Jay their senior? Is Jay their classmate? Oh God! How old is Jay? Why do I not know such a simple and important thing about my business partner.

Am I young enough to date someone his age?

"Wait! I never understood why the two of you ran away from home!" I look at the twins for answers.

"Our father was stalking us. He wanted us to go back home with him. He kept threatening us, saying that he would hurt our mother, if we did not go back with him. So, we left home. There was no other way to protect mom and aunt Cee Cee."

Cee Cee! So that's what the twins call the younger woman. Cee Cee and her Caramel Cappuccino! That should help me remember her name.

I do wonder if the twins know her real name. They must, right? Because, Cee Cee sounds like a nickname or a pseudonym. So, maybe they are just habituated with one of her aliases?

These women have had to hide for so long. The detective did say that they have been using different aliases to stay hidden for nearly a decade now. But, their unhinged husband still managed to find them.

"Thanks for letting me know that Jay is back in town. That's one less thing for me to worry about. And I guess I'll be waiting for him to meet me!" I smile, awkwardly. Or, maybe it is melodramatic. But I definitely sounded a little desperate.

Ah! Who cares? I don't think I'll be meeting the twins that often. My embarrassment can't possibly be the highlight of our very first conversation.

"You're welcome!" the twins rush towards me and hug me. I may not know them that well but, the hug feels like home.

Does everyone feel like home, when you feel lonely enough to let anyone show you affection?

"I should head back. There is a lunch commitment and I might be running a little late already!" I get off the couch and head towards the door.

The twins ask me to come back again and visit them, since we stay close to one another. They seem friendly. But, I'm not sure about it. What could we possibly talk about? The only reason I stayed for so long was to know more about Jay. They might get bored of my outdated topics of conversation, if I keep showing up too often.

"Don't forget about the birthday party, next week!" the women remind me, as I wave goodbye from the elevator. And, once I press the overused button for the lobby, the metal door gently closes between us.

I check a text on my phone that reads "I'm here!".

Am I actually running late for lunch? We do have a reservation. But the elevator keeps stopping at every other floor and takes forever to get to the lobby.

Sophie is waiting in her car, arguing with the doorman and insisting that I'll be out, any moment now. It's cute. I know she will always fight for me.

"I'm here! I'm here! Let's go! Sorry for taking so long!" I quickly hop into the car as I apologize to the doorman.

"We will miss our reservation!" Sophie yells at me and I laugh.

"It's just a few blocks away. We will make it."

Thankfully, the restaurant had valet parking because, Sophie was right! We might have missed our reservation if we did not make it to the hostess desk on time. The place is packed, more densely than it usually is on a usual Friday afternoon. They would have giving away our table to someone else.

"Finally! I'm starting. Let's order before we talk!" Sophie looks through the menu.

"I'll have what you're having!" I say while looking at the wine menu. It's good that we have the same taste in food and drinks.

And, before I can pick a drink for us, Sophie hides behind the menu and casually says something that I've never heard her say ever since we first met.

"Wait! I'll skip the wine."

"What? Why? Are you okay?"

"Um...yeah! Just no wine, okay?" she hides a smile.

"AM I GOING TO BE AN AUNT?" I almost yell with excitement.

"Hush! It's too soon. Wait for the official announcement like everyone else!" she smiles from behind the menu and I smile back in a way that she understands how I feel.

Wow! She will be such a good mom. She will fight the World to make sure her kid is safe and happy. I'm so happy for her. What should I buy for her kid? Maybe I can be the cool aunt and spoil her, or him. Oh God! This is so exciting!

"Did the detective call you?" her question pulls me back to reality.

"Yeah! He said that the vandal case has been closed because Jay dropped the charges. And the attack case was dismissed, since the man pleaded on the grounds of temporary insanity! Are you okay? How do you feel about it?"

"I'm mad at them for dismissing the case so easily. But they claim that I'm safe and the man is in some rehab facility. I want to punch that psychopath. But I guess it's pointless to fight a mentally unstable person. I just hope that he stops hurting people." Sophie sighs. That was a mature response. Why did I expect her to be more angry than she is, at this moment? Maybe she has matured more than I have. I'm still mad at that man. And I'm definitely mad at Jay. But for what? He was just trying to help everyone.

"I'm sorry about everything that happened to you because of me and my business partner." I apologize to her.

"It was never your fault. You were reeled into this, just like I was. But I'm just glad that you're safe now." Sophie caresses my hand as she looks for the waitress to place our order.

"Excuse me? Can someone please take our order?"

"Of course, ma'am!" the waitress rushes towards us. And she assures us to get the order read soon, before leaving with the menus.

Lunch arrives, faster than usual, or maybe we talk about so many things that time just flies. Sophie asks me if I've heard from Jay. I ask her about life with her notorious in-laws. We both argue about who is having a harder time before devouring our meal.

Wow! Maybe I was hungrier than I thought I was. This is the first time I enjoyed my lunch in a while. Maybe it was a good idea to visit the women and get to meet the twins.

I wonder what Jay is doing, right now.

Sophie drives me back to my apartment and asks "Do you want me to stay for some time?".

I smile and reply "You need to get back home and rest. Don't make my ex-neighbor come back here and yell at me.".

We laugh about how over-protective Sophie's partner is, and always will be. And, after a second remind from my doorman, asking Sophie to move the car away from the entrance, she finally let's me step out of her car.

"I'll see you again, next week, right?" Sophie asks while waving. And I smile before replying "See you soon!".

The apartment feels empty as I drag my feet and walk in. The sun is setting and the warmth is slowly fading away, leaving the walls cold and lonely, just like me. I change into something comfortable and turn on the TV. There is nothing interesting to watch but the sights and sounds keep me company. And before I know it, the clock reads half past twelve. Was I watching TV for so long? I must have been lost in my thoughts.

There is nothing much to do anymore. So I get off the couch and set my bed for a long slumber.

The cafe is supposed to reopen on the coming Monday. Our maintenance work will take another day and the cleaning crew will need half a day to get the place ready for customers again. The intern is working from a satellite kitchen, throughout the weekend, to fulfill the deliveries for all the bakery pre-orders, until we reopen.

He definitely deserves a full-time position. The way he single-handedly managed all the pre-orders, this morning, was phenomenal. He has been extremely helpful throughout the month. We should promote him on the upcoming Anniversary of our cafe. Everyone is set to get a bonus and I hope that he will want to keep working with us, even after completing his internship.

"There's so much to do! Oh My God! I really need my partner back!" I yell out loud for no one but my walls to hear.

After turning the TV off and dragging myself off the couch, I remind myself that I'll probably be living inside my bedroom for the entirety of the weekend. So, I grab some smacks, a bottle of water and a few extra pillows from the hallway storage.

The snack packets make so much noise as I try to make them stand on my bedside table, right next to the bottle of water. The pillows need to be meticulously placed because, my stressed mind needs to be over organized, just to feel a little better, somehow.

I double check if my front door is locked before I tuck myself into my comfortable little fortress-in-bed. But, it still feels empty, even with the extra pillows laying in a neat line, right next to me.

Why did Jay not tell me about his plan? Was he even obligated to? Why did he just leave so suddenly?

I miss him!

knock knock knock

"What the heck?" I yell, as I pull myself out of my comfy bed. The clock reads 1 AM and I worry who it could possibly be at this time of the night.

"Who is it?" I ask with a baseball bat in my hand. It's unsettling and I don't want to open the door.

"It's me!" a familiar voice replies. But, I'm not sure.

"And who the heck is ME?" I ask, trying to sound a little scary. "I have the local PD detective on speed dial. Go away, before I call him."

"That's great! Call him, now! He couldn't have gotten too far. We were having drinks together before he dropped me home."

I'm so mad at Jay, right now.

I put the bat down and open the door, just enough to peak into the hallway. And, just like the first time he came over, I see a pair of doe eyes, staring back at me. He still looks beautiful, even when he looks a little tired. His smile is still as bright as it was when he left. The sparkle in his eyes are still the same.

"Why are you here?" I ask him.

"I missed you! Didn't you miss me?"

"Go home!"

"I am home!"

This is so annoying. I want to punch him right now.

The safety chair rattles when I pull it out and open the door. And, after a little hesitation, Jay asks "Can I come in?".

"Hmmm! Come in!"

I put the bat back in my bedroom while Jay closes the door behind him.

"Were you going to hit me, with that?" he asks with a mischievous look on his face. His annoyingly pretty finger is pointing toward my room at the spot where I kept the bat. But, his curious eyes are fixated on me, for once.

"I still might so, don't be too annoying. TALK! Where were you and why did you ignore me for so long?"

"I had to settle everything before coming back!"

"Keep giving cryptic answers and I'll go get the bat!"

"Sit with me! I'll tell you everything, promise!"

We sit on the couch and he start talking about how it was all connected to him and his family. The vandalism, the attack and even the twins.

"That man is my father's half brother. His parents were separated just a few years after he was born. My grandfather left his home town to settle here, with a much wealthier woman. Her family invested in his ideas and he quickly earned a fortune. My father, her first born, was given a childhood that most kids, in his generation, could only dream of."

A quick pause that follows, is filled with a sense of disappointment, or disgust. His lips twitch for a second and his brows meet, just for a second. But, he clears his throat and continues while his brows ease back to their usual position.

"And, while my family had it all, that man spent his entire childhood, trying to make ends meet. Even his mother decided to leave him, soon after her separation with my grandfather. He kept telling everyone that he had no one, no family, no parents. It was easier than explaining to people that his parents had abandoned him. Every relationship in his life was eventually and inevitably effected by the way his parents treated him." Jay pauses, again.

I look into his eyes, wondering if he needs a reply from me. Or, if he needs me to comfort him. But I'm confused.

Because, it's a lot to take in. I don't know how to react to his family history when I have only barely started to know him.

"Should I get to the point?" he asks me and I shrug. At this point, nothing seems impossible. That man seems to have been through a lot. And maybe, so has Jay. So it might make sense for Jay to help him.

"Eventually, he found out about my father, and then, about me. And he started stalking the cafe and all of us. He was resentful. He wanted the life that my father has. He wanted his kids to have the life that I have. If only he knew that I'm an outcast, just like he is." Jay sounds sad. The pain in his voice somehow resonates with me.

I used to think that his parents loved him. But maybe, he grew up to be such a beautifully kind person, in spite of his environment and upbringing. A kind and beautiful man, with so much to offer the world, someone who looks so sad and vulnerable, every time he talks about the past.

Maybe, that's what we have in common! Maybe, our painful pasts drive us to find comfort in one another.

But, I don't even know how to react, right now. It's confusing! Should I hold him? Should I hold his hand? Do hugs heal him, just like they heal me?

I decide to pick the simplest option and hold his hand. And, when my fingers wrap around his fist, he looks at me with warmth sparking in his big, beautiful eyes.

"You don't have to talk about it, unless you want to!" I remind him that he does not need to hurt himself, just to clarify things for me.

"I want to. You need to know this. You're a part of my life, aren't you?" he asks and I nod. Because, I am, right? I am his business partner, if nothing else. We work together, everyday.

He continues "The man spotted his wives at the cafe, one day. It was pure luck that he bumped into them while stalking us. But he grew even more resentful. He thought that we were helping his family stay away from him. So, he did all the things he did, thinking that he had nothing to loose and a lot to gain. He thought he could have his family back by making sure that they had nowhere else to go."

"That's cynical!" I cringe.

"It's the only way he could think of. Everyone kept leaving him. I don't blame him for becoming cynical. He spent all that time without the children he loved so much. Whatever he had saved, whatever he managed to earn, was spent in trying to find his children. And when he did find them, he realized that they didn't even love him anymore. It would break me, if I went looking for someone, for so long, just to be rejected again!"

Maybe, Jay is right. Maybe, he understands that man because he too feels left out. Maybe, he grew up with comfort that comes from wealth and not from affection.

Paying for his comfort or making sure he does not get into any trouble, is not the same as loving him. Maybe, they protect Jay out of obligation, for the sake of their family name.

"I'm sorry you have had to go through all this, because of me and my family!" he holds my hands in his and gives them a squeeze. His grasp on them is so tight that it slightly hurts my fingers. But, I can't pull away, not when he seems so upset. All of this, seems a little too personal, for him. He is trying to make amends where he did no wrong. He is doing all this for his people, for his family.

"It's okay! We are okay! Don't worry! I'm okay!" I assure him and he loosens his grip on my hands.

"Hey, Jay? How did you find out about all this?"

"I recognized the quote that the man carved into our cafe table! It's something my grandfather used to say to my father and then to me and my little brother while we were growing up. So, I knew that it had to be linked to my family, somehow."

"Oh! But why didn't you tell me about any of this, before you left?"

"I didn't want you to leave. Maybe, I'm just like him. I did not want to give people a reason to leave me. And please, believe me when I say that, I may sympathize with him but I do not condone his actions. I'm sorry for what happened to

Sophie. She was nothing but kind to me, to all of us, and I let her down. And I hope that she can forgive me."

"It's okay! She won't blame you for any of it."

"I'll make it up to her, I promise!" Jay assures me, and I nod. Because, I believe him. I know he will make sure that Sophie gets over her traumatic experience. And, now that she is starting a new phase of life, I think she might be far more forgiving, once she gets to know the whole story.

"Is that man okay now? Will he be fine?" I ask him as I slide my hands out of his grasp. My palms feel sweaty and it's slightly embarrassing.

"I'll make sure he does not suffer anymore. He will be meeting his kids, next month. He seems to be doing well at rehab. I have faith in him. I know, deep down, he wants to change. He just misses his kids!"

There is such strong belief in his eyes, when he says those things, about a man who almost ruined everything for him. It makes me want to know everything that's hurting him. He must feel broken enough to want others to heal.

"That's good news, I guess!" I try to understand his point of view, even when I do not fully agree with it, at least not until I see that man making any progress.

"Oh and apparently, Cee Cee, the woman who helped the twins and their mom, her name is Cee Cee." Jay gently chuckles, and I nod. It's nice to see him find something sweet and amusing, again.

"And, she has her whole family here. They are living nearby, just a few miles down south from the city limits. She asked Kay to help her smooth things over with her brother and her parents. So, I'm thinking of sending them on a mini vacation. They could use some quality time together." Jay smiles, fondly.

"Did you really just plan on sending a stranger and her family, on a vacation?"

"Yup! They deserve one! She has been feeling guilty about ruining everything for the twins. And, she has been punishing herself by staying away from her own family. And, her family have been so respectful of her wishes. They have been keeping an eye from a distance but giving her space to deal with her life, on her own. I think that's very admirable!" he pouts, resisting a smile. His eyes keeps looking away from me and his twitching lips hold him back from giving any more explanations.

But, I think it makes him feel proud to know that he is about to do the right thing. And, it looks adorable.

He tucks a few rogue strands of his hair, behind his ear, and pushes the rest back with his palm. And, I can't stop thinking about the fact that my sweaty hands were in his, just a few seconds ago.

Is he really not embarrassed by anything? Does nothing bother him? Because, I didn't even see him wipe his hands dry before running it through his luscious hair.

Do I really not bother him, at all?

"Hey! Are you glad that I'm back?" he asks and I nod.

The smile on his face is brighter than all the lights in my living room. And, I seriously wonder if he is real or just a figment of my imagination. Everything about him is comforting, somehow. And, it makes me want to take care of him, even if he did not ask for it, even if he might not need me to.

As I map his face, I notice that his lips have run dry from talking for such a long time. But, they keep calling out to me and making me want to kiss him. He says something but I'm zoned out from the conversation. My focus is fixated on his lips.

gasp

Water! I should get him some water!

"You know what, Jay? I knew you could not be a bad guy! You could not possibly be THAT BAD!" I chuckle as I get off the couch. Maybe I can muster my courage and kiss him on another day.

"THAT BAD? So you did think that I'm a little bad, huh?"

"Maybe?" I grab a glass from the kitchen cabinet and try hiding my flushed face while filling it with water.

"Hey! Can I stay here, tonight?" Jay asks while walking towards the kitchen. His footsteps inch closer and closer. I almost hope that he holds me, hugs me, or maybe rests his head on my shoulder, again. But, he does no such thing.

Instead, he catches one of my sticky notes, just as the piece of paper began it's unscheduled flight. I might have brushed too close to it and peeled it off while getting the glass from a cabinet. And, as he sticks the note, back to it's original place, I can almost hear my inner voice screaming with joy.

As I hide my excitement and hand him the glass, my lips barely manage to say "Drink this! You've been talking for way too long!".

He smiles, so innocently, before slowly gulping down, savoring it. And all I can think about is that he even drinks like the cutest person to have ever existed among mere mortals.

How can a man like him, be interested in me?

He must be. He is here, right? He called it home, not my home but, home. Just home!

HOME!

He feels like he belongs here. So, he must feel like he belongs with me, right? Because, right now, I do feel like I belong with him!

"Thank you! That was very refreshing!" he smiles and sets the glass down on the kitchen counter. And, before I can react, he gently holds my hand and he pulls me out of the kitchen. We walk past the coffee table and the couch before finally halting next to the bookshelf that holds my precious vinyl records.

"Can I play something, for us?" he asks and, I nod.

And, of course, he picks the most romantic song.

As the song softly plays, he holds my hands again and asks "Can I hug you?". And, what am I supposed to say? No? When I'm aching to be in his arms? When I'm desperately missing his touch? When I'm too much of a coward to ask for a hug?

I'm so happy that he asked!

We hold each other and gently move with the music. It seems like forever since I've felt his touch. And I don't even notice what time it is but, the night is slowly fading away.

Did we just spend the entire night talking about his past? *Fascinating!*

"I missed this! I missed home!" Jay mumbles, next to my ear, as soon as his chin rests on my shoulder.

"We have never danced like this before. And you have stayed here just once." I protest and instantly regret my tone. Maybe I should have thought before I replied to his gentle statement.

But, instead of being offended, he chuckles and replies "Home is any place where you are around! The cafe, your apartment, my place, anywhere!".

"Did your house feel empty without me?" I ask, gently. And, he nods into my neck. My arms want to hold him close, tighter. But, before I can act on that thoughts, he is firmly pulling me closer.

Is this domestic? It feels domestic.

"Hey! You never answered my question!" he asks when he pulls back, just a little, to look into my eyes.

And, what am I supposed to do, when he looks at me so affectionately? His doe eyes have superpowers.

"Stay, for as long as you want!" I pull him back into the hug and he rests his chin on my shoulder, again, pressing in with his weight and melting into my arms.

His weight on me, feels like home!

I can hear his breathing even out and he doesn't seem anxious anymore.

"Oh! By the way, I have to tell you something. And I know it may seem like a joke but, it's not. And it's kind of important." he mumbles, next to my ear.

"Yeah? What's that?" I ask as he pulls back again and looks at me with those sparking eyes of his.

"My name isn't J-A-Y Jay! It's actually just the letter J!" he chuckles. And I'm not sure if he is joking or actually being serious.

"What? Seriously?"

"Yup! Sorry for taking so long to talk about it!"

I want to smack him for taking too long to talk about everything. But, I also want to smack myself for not knowing almost anything about him.

"Why did you not correct me sooner?" I smack his shoulder and he pretends like it hurt, a lot.

"Usually, I never do. My name is complicated! The letter J, as a name, seems a little confusing. So, I just go along with Jay. Plus, most people know nothing about me. But, I want you to know me, all of me."

He looks like he is testing me with his doe eyes. And, I can blame him all I want. But, I've never actually bothered to look into the papers that we signed, when we started working together.

We both had lawyers who were looking into every important detail. And, all I had to do was sign the paperwork. His name was always Jay in the cafe register. So, I went along with it.

I almost certain that even Sophie does not knows his real name. Or maybe she does? And maybe I need to start reading things properly, before I sign them.

"Can I know your full name?" I ask and he whispers it into my ear. His warm breath is almost distracting. His hands are holding my arms and pull me closer as he whisper. It's almost too enticing. But, I still manage to hear it, even when I don't fully understand it.

I want to know what it means. I want to know everything about him. And maybe, someday, I'll tell him everything about me.

"WOW! That is definitely complicated!" I chuckle and he laughs before he says "Told you! And that's exactly why Jay makes more sense around here!".

We look into each other's eyes, waiting for the other to say something, anything. And I watch his lips curl into a big smile that speaks volumes.

Oh, his smile! I missed his smile. His kind, bright and welcoming smile. And I want to make him smile, for the rest of his life.

The music keeps playing and we keep dancing, until we see the sun near the horizon. Eventually, the warmth of a new day, slowly fills the apartment. The walls are suddenly smiling again, glittering under the rays of the early morning sun. Their is hope in the air, again. My sticky notes are cheerfully dancing with the breeze, again.

The morning has just arrived and today's mood is already filled with a new feeling that I can't fully describe, at least not with just a few words. It's beautiful and magical, maybe even a little surreal. And, it's something that can only be felt, experienced.

"Can I keep calling you Jay?" I ask him, when we are back on the couch. And he nods with a gentle, flickering smile on his face. I'm certain that he is hiding his sleep deprivation behind the glowing joy of coming back home. And, I keep holding him as he melts into the couch to inevitably doze off.

Maybe, we can just sleep in?

We have the entire weekend to ourselves. And honestly, I like how we are tangled, right now. His arms are caging me in and my weight is on his shoulder. But, he isn't nagging about it. All he is doing is pulling me further into his grasp, that is strong, even when he is half asleep.

It's intoxicating.

His chest is gently rocking under my cheek. The way he is breathing, makes me think of soft ocean waves that gently kiss the shoreline, just as the sun kisses the horizon.

It makes me believe that I can finally heal from every trauma that I have hidden behind my smiles.

I might never understand how, someone like him, even thinks of me in the way that he does. I wonder what gives him the strength to adore someone filled with so many doubts and fears. But, I will learn to accept the perks that come with an affectionate, dare I say, non-platonic partner.

WOW! I never thought that I'd call him anything, other than my business partner. But, here I am, in his arms, dozing off on his chest while he gently snores.

And yes, it's definitely my couch that makes him snore. I can hear the rumbling sounds under my ear, as I doze off. Maybe, we can move to the bedroom after we wake up. And maybe, we wouldn't need as many pillows as we did last time.

I used to believe that a home is where you feel safe, within the confines of brick walls. Perhaps, a home is a person who can make you feel safe, anywhere, anytime.

I think I've finally found my home!

EPILOGUE

It's always a surprisingly bright day, right after a gloomy night. The rain has cleared the skies and the sun feels especially warm. A sea of people are walking down the block while I navigate the narrow pedestrian lane that leads to the cafe.

The mesmerizing fragrances from a nearby flower shop, has filled the air with a faint sense of comfort. The metal gates of the cafe, have been wide open for hours and there are dozens of people occupying the outdoor seating.

I can hear the rhythmic clicking and tapping of keyboards as I walk together the entrance. And I wonder if Jay ever reconsidered turning the cafe into a community work space, like he wanted to, before the partnership was finalized.

The glass doors of the cafe, are closed for entry, since the place is packed to the brim. So, I pull out my phone and try calling her. And, as soon as the call connects, I can see her standing behind the counter, looking at the screen of her phone before looking around the cafe. I wave at her to grab her attention and she gestures, asking me to wait outside. So, I do!

I take a seat, right next to the table that started it all. The carving has since been fixed, masked to the best of someone's ability. It's like the words were never engraved and the rage was never expressed. I heard that the man was doing well and had met his family. The twins are still mad at him but they are trying. After all, everyone tries to adjust, when it's family. We all try, even when it hurts us and leaves a scar that almost never fully heals.

I pat myself to check if my diary is still in my pocket. It's barely the size of my palm but it feels heavier than it should. I've never brought it out, in public. It usually lives inside a dark drawer of my bedside table. But, maybe I'll have the courage to give it to her, if she forgives me.

"Hey! Sorry to keep you waiting, detective! Shall we?" she smiles, half heartedly, as she steps out of the cafe. So, I simply nod before getting off the seat and start walking alongside her.

"The cafe is doing really well!" I trying to ease us into a conversation with a genuine complement.

"Yeah! The Anniversary Celebration rush and all the SALE promotions from last week, have been really helpful. That temp barista we hired for the week, to handle the rush, is a marketing wiz."

"That's great!" I smile as we keep waking ahead.

"So, where are we headed?" she asks as we walk past an ocean of pedestrians who are walking in every possible direction. Their footstep keep echoing in my head and reminding me of the past. But, I try not to let that effect me.

I look towards her and say "There's a deli down the block that makes amazing sandwich! I think you might like it."

"I like sandwich! But, we could have had those in the cafe itself!" she chuckles. It's nice to see her being cheerful about something. Maybe, that half-hearted smile earlier, was not from annoyance or disgust but from exhaustion. Maybe, she doesn't hate me. Maybe, she doesn't even remember me.

"Ah! Well, I don't think I can afford those sandwich with my salary."

"I could say that it would be on-the-house but, I wouldn't want to offend you." she says, politely, while looking at the stop sign. The display reads 37 seconds. So, we wait in silence while hundreds of cars pass us by.

When the pedestrian light turns green, we cross the street with a sea of people, right next to us. Some bump into me and some bump into her as we walk ahead. And, after we have successfully crossed the bustling road, the sandwich shop is finally visible.

"There! That's the one!" I say while pointing at the rustic sign board. You can barely read the name but the sign board itself has become an integral part of the neighborhood.

"Oh! I've been here before. They make the best Tuna Melt and BLT!" she smiles, sincerely. It makes me happy to have picked this place. And, it makes me happy that she agreed to have lunch with me.

We place our order and grab a seat, right next to the exit. There are only a handful of tables in this joint. But, it feels cozy, almost like someone's home.

"So? What are we here for?" she asks while fiddling with the menu card that it slid into an old, plastic stand. The menu card isn't entirely legible. But, no one even uses it anymore. People just order from the menu boards near the cash register.

Yet, come rain or shine, through sauce spills and ketchup kerfuffles, the menu cards are always there, on every table. And, just like the sign board, the menu cards have seen better days. But, it's all a part of the charm. And maybe, it even adds to the dining experience.

"Sandwiches! We are here for sandwiches!"

I'm nervous! I don't know how to start the conversation. I've never been so nervous about anything else in my life. Moreover, I don't want her to think that I'm hitting on her.

This is absurd and slightly terrifying. How do I ask her if she remembers me? And, if she does, how do I ask her to forgive me?

"Of course! Sandwiches are great!" she replies while looking out of the window and adds "But, I'm sure you had something else in mind when you asked me to meet you for lunch, instead of asking Jay!".

"Ah! Yes! Well, I'm not sure if you remember this but we have met before, in college. In fact, you were one of our TA. Remember? Professor Ian's freshmen batch? We were in his last freshmen batch before he decide to focus only on the seniors."

"Hmmm. I remember him. And, I remember you! You used to be a lot chunkier back then, just like I was. Well, I still am!" she softly chuckles as her gaze shifts focus from the bustling streets to my sweaty brows before she adds "And, you were suffocated by the smell of cigarettes, just like I was!".

Her smile slowly fades before another one reappears, masking her deepest feelings. But, the smile isn't enough to calm my racing heart. Because, she remembers me! The realization makes me heart pound like a beating drum! The vein on my forehead is pulsating a bit too fast.

Is it too late to throw myself out of the window and run away?

No!
I must focus!

This is my chance! I have been waiting for this moment for such a long time. I have prepared an apology speech that I can't remember anymore. But, it must be done! I must power through.

"I'm sorry for what happened that day, near the old A/V room on campus. And, I'm really sorry for running away."

When I can't meet her eyes anymore, it feels like I'm back in that basement bathroom and there is smoke in the air. And, I'm feeling suffocated, all over again.

"That was a long time ago. I try not to think about it. And you shouldn't worry about it either." her voice sounds neutral and get words sound sincere. But, there is an unsettling silence that follows her assurance, until our order arrives.

The sandwiches fill the air with a warm, toasty feeling. But, I wonder if I even deserve it. I wonder if I deserve to feel relieved, so easily.

"Let's share?" she asks and I nod.

I watch her wipe her hands with a napkin that she pulls out of her pants pocket. And she proceeds to gently separate the two halves of both sandwiches. She delicately sets down one half of each sandwich on our plates and it now looks like the triangular design on top of a fortress wall. Both halves are standing next to one another and shining under the bright overhead bulbs that real should have been turned off in the afternoon.

The fillings are visible now and the crispy edges look scrumptious. Our sandwiches look even more delicious that they did, just a few seconds ago. And, I wonder if that why their cafe has such expensive dishes. Appetizing plating and attention to details. Or maybe it's the love that they serve it with.

Can love add flavor to a dish?

I must focus on the task in hand. I must apologize, again. This is too easy. She can't possibly forgive me so easily. I must try harder.

"I'm sorry it took me so long to find you and ask for your forgiveness."

"It's fine! I don't hold a grudge against you. That bully, however, is on my list!" she laughs.

"How did you get out of there, after I ran away?"

She smiles while gesturing for me to start eating, and says "I have my ways!".

I quickly take a bite off a crispy corner and ask "Does Jay know about it?".

"No! And I wish to keep it that way. He has done enough! We wouldn't want to worry him, would we?"

"Not at all! And, I understand. My lips are sealed! But please, forgive me for what happened that day!"

"It was not your fault! You were just a kid! At least you are doing the right thing with your life, right now! I'm sure you've been helping many people out there."

She looks around and grabs a bottle of ketchup from the empty table next to us. The way she twists the lid off and hits the bottom with her palm, makes the hair behind my neck, stand in fear.

Is that something she does with more than just a bottle? Is that how she got out of that basement; aggression, self defense, dominance?

"And, weren't you a victim as well?" she asks while setting the bottle down and dipping a corner of her sandwich into the pool of ketchup on her plate. The red liquid is smeared easily under the slightest of pressure, until it coats the crispy surface.

As she takes a delicate bite, the melted cheese oozes out and lands on the plate. And, as she keeps chewing, the sounds keep getting louder and louder.

Am I having another panic attack?

She look at me with concern in her gaze as she asks "Didn't he bully almost everyone on campus? Didn't his lackeys try to strangle you for not making me obey him? Didn't they chase you around for the rest of the academic year, until they graduated?".

She pauses to take another bite, savors it, and continues talking. "You think I left but, I just stopped working for the Professor, just to avoid those spoiled brats. But, I knew what they were doing. Who do you think filed a complaint after they locked those freshmen inside the gym?" she smiles, softly.

I sigh before responding "You always looked out for us but none of us did anything to make your life any easier!".

"What nonsense? I loved working with Professor Ian, because of you guys. Most of you were so polite and kind to me. And it is foolish to fight bullies who go to great lengths, just to hurt people. I'm glad you did not get involved. And, I honestly have such fond memories from being a TA. So, I choose to focus only on the good things from that part of my life!"

She gestures again and asks me to continue eating. And, I'm almost certain that it's the biggest reason why she gets along with Jay. Because, they are both always wanting to take care of everyone around them.

"Do you really forgive me? So easily?" I ask and she says "There isn't anything to forgive but, if it helps, I forgive you!". There is a kind smile on her face. And, I want to say something. I want to thank her. I want to give her my diary. I want to tell her how she has lifted a huge weight of my shoulders. But, her phone starts to ring.

"Excuse me! And please, eat up!" she says before pulling out her phone from her back pocket and accepting the call.

Her conversation runs long enough for me to finish my sandwich and order myself another one. It's been so long since I've had a peaceful meal. Somehow, talking to her has made my appetite come back. And, I think I can finally live again.

"Sorry about that!" she says after hanging up. *"It was Jay and he wanted to join. I hope it's okay that I told him where we are, right now!"*

"Of course! More the merrier. I just ordered another sandwich!" I am rambling, unable to contain my excitement. And, she smiles, fondly.

I hope she can finally move on and, so can I. It will be nice to have a full night's rest without having another nightmare.

"Thank you for forgiving me!" I feel relaxed, as I say the words out loud. And, she nods.

"You know you can count on me, right?" I look into her kind eyes that truly seem to have no grudge in them, at least for me. And, she nods again, with a sincere smile.

I feel relieved, revived!

Jay arrives, just as my sandwich does. And, as always, he grabs it before I can even smell the warm, toasty fragrance.

But, he is just too precious for me to protest. We have practically grown up together. So, he can have anything he wants. What's mine is his. For better or for worse, we are twined together by fate!

"How's Ms. Park-View Penthouse?" I ask and Jay laughs before replying *"Sophie is fine! We are heading upstate, this weekend, for her 70s themed housewarming party. She has finally, fully settled in."*

"That's nice! Now she can enjoy an ocean view!"

Jay softly chuckles before saying "You should join us! That way, you can use a few of those paid leaves that you keep piling up. Plus, they have a massive wine cellar. You'll love it!".

"Ah! Sounds fun! Count me in!" I smile. It would be interesting to go back inside those obnoxiously opulent, gated communities, without the badge.

My last trip upstate was with a few dozen squad cars, a canine unit and the biggest forensic team I have ever worked with. But, that was a few years ago and I'm sure that the residents have forgotten all about it. They don't exactly remember people like me, not unless we disrupt their lives. And, even when we do, they find a way to push the past aside and move on.

We had an absurd misunderstanding when we were trying to solve that case. One of the neighbors, a couple of houses away from the crime scene, was hosting a private event. And, he assumed that our squad was mooching off him, through his caterer.

We were certainly not trying to feed our squad on his dime. In reality, we were just ambushed by an extremely empathetic man with the most innocent eyes. And what were we supposed to do, when we were all working for hours under the summer sun on an empty stomach?

I remember how the caterer came over and asked our captain, if he could get some snacks for the squad. And, I remember how it made him look suspicious. But, he still tried to do something, anything to help.

That was the day when I reconnect with Jay, years after graduating from high school. People called it a coincidence. They said that it was pure luck that my high school friend was catering for an event, right next to the biggest crime scene of the year.

But, I don't think that any of it was a coincidence. I reconnected with him as he started working with a new business partner. And, the vandal found his way to us, right when I found my way back to her.

I'm just glad that I could help, as little as I did. I'm glad that everyone is safe and finally back home, with the people who love them. And, I do think I was barely useful because Jay did all the heavy lifting.

He always tries to help everyone. He always puts his neck on the line for others. I know for a fact that everyone feels safe around him. His energy can heal you, somehow. And, I know for a fact that she too, will be safe with him.

Jay's family is just as notoriously powerful as Sophie's soon-to-be in-laws or their snobby, snack-counting neighbors. He can make or break people with the snap of his fingers. Yet, he chooses to be gentle. He choose to be chivalrous.

Of course, his chivalry walks out of the door when he sees my sandwich and eat it all, without sharing even a little bit, not even the dry, over-toasted corner that has turned black. Yet, his face is glowing like the brightest summer sun that's gliding through the clear blue sky.

How is his face always so, so innocent? He still looks like he did, back when we first met, years ago. He is still a big baby in a butch, gentleman's form.

Does he have to be so magnificent? Because, it makes us look bad, like we don't even try to comb our hair and iron our shirt.

Wait! Did I iron my shirt, this morning?

Random thoughts aside, I'm still hungry! Maybe I should order another sandwich? Or maybe I should head back to the station and finish my work for the day, so that I can go back home, a little early. I haven't done that before. Going back home was never a fun thing to do. Who would want to stay up all night, alone, with nothing but his own thoughts?

This is the first time when I'm looking forward to anything other than work. It's nice to have my appetite back. And, I hope to finally get a good night's rest, now that I have finally made amends.

I can finally move on from my past. And I hope she can keep smiling, just like she does, every time she looks into Jay's gentle and glittering eyes.

Maybe, he is made this way, perfect in every sense, just for her. Because, that's what she deserved. So, the universe made him, just for her.

"Hey?" Jay waves at me from the cash register. I didn't even realize that he got off his seat and went there, while I was busy talking to myself.

"Do you want something else? My treat!" he adds, after I look towards him, still dazed, still processing the thoughts that I was having. So, I get off my seat and walk towards the cashier. The menu board is legible, only when you read it from a short distance.

This place is just like us, barely functional, always nostalgic and craving for some love and attention.

"Yeah! I do!" I finally answer, while pointing at a sandwich on the menu board, that I haven't tried yet.

It seems like the right time to try something new. And who knows, maybe I'll find something new to look forward to, every time I revisit this place.

"Let's go!" Jay nudges me towards the pick up counter after paying the bill. It will take a few minutes to get the order ready but, I follow his lead. Moreover, I want to use this moment with him, to ask an important question.

"Hey! I wanted to ask you something!"

"Sure! Ask away!" Jay smiles.

"Do you like her?" I question him, while we get pushed and shoved by a couple of hungry men who are trying to collect their order. It's funny how humans behave, when we are hungry.

Jay turns his head towards our table and looks at her with the most gentle expression as he replies *"I love her!"*.

Yup! He is definitely made for her. No wonder he never found someone he could be with, for more than a week.

I'm so happy for him. He has finally found someone who completes him. And, I really hope that he does not make the same mistakes that his family did.

As I watch our sandwiches being prepared, Jay keep turning around to face our table. His eyes fondly fixate on her while she looks outside the window, embracing the view. The buildings are glittering under an unusually bright sun. Her eyes keep tracing the shapes of the structures ahead. And, even when she has no idea that Jay is looking at her, her body somehow reacts to him. Her shoulders are not tense anymore. She isn't restlessly tapping her feet anymore. Even her soft smile seems warmer and more real, somehow.

I tap my pocket to check if my diary is still in it. And, after a quick conformation, I decide not to give it to her. She seems happy, just like Jay is. And, it does feel like she has moved on from that awful part of our past. So, maybe it's time for me to do the same.

When we head back to our table with our sandwiches, we talk about random things, about life and about the plans for the weekend. And soon, it is time to get back to work.

After I wave goodbye to them, they walk towards the cafe and I head towards to the station. We slowly inch away from each other as we walk in opposite directions. But, I do look back to make sure that they are okay. And I see her, wrapped in his arms, glittering like the brightest star in the night sky.

They are patiently waiting for the pedestrian lights to turn green. The intersection ahead of them, is packed with rush-hour traffic. Commuters must be heading back to work after lunch, just like us.

She looks so calm when he places a gentle kiss on her forehead. And, it's an annoyingly beautiful sight.

I wonder if I'll ever have something like that.
I hope that I find something similar, someday.

Because, now that I have been forgiven,
I think I deserve a second chance at love.

With that thought, I turn around and start walking towards the station, again. There is a desk full of pending paperwork, waiting for me. But, I'm smiling.

My shoulders do not feel heavy anymore. The dull headache, that always lurked around, isn't there anymore.

What a day!

I was extremely worried when it began. And now, I feel nothing but joy, hope and freedom. I can finally move on from my past.

The wind feels refreshingly cold when I Inhale, deeply, consciously. The burning sensation in my chest, the memories of the smokey basement, are not weighing down on me anymore.

The sea of people are not noisy anymore. Their never-ending footstep are not echoing inside my head anymore. The voices of self judgement, much like the headache, aren't lingering nor asking me to prove my worth in this World.

Nothing is suffocating me anymore.
I can finally and freely breathe again.

I understand it now!
Healing feels beautiful!

ACKNOWLEDGEMENT

I am thrilled to dedicated, my third book of this series, to all those who believe in me, love me and support my creations. This series, that started as a part of my creative bucket-list, has received so much love from all across the globe. I'm extremely grateful for all the kind reviews, motivating feedbacks and heart-warning cheers. My readers are my pride and I am so lucky to have your support.

This book is dedicated to everyone who treats people with empathy and kindness, even when their own struggles are not always visible to others. Health and wellness has been a big part of my social initiatives and it certainly includes mental well-being. I hope that this story and this series, helps you understand and empathize with people facing trauma, bullying or any other form of stress. And, if you faced it yourself, I applaud your strength and celebrate the beauty that you add to our lives.

A special thanks to my Parents, my Family, my Digital Family and of course my amazing Notion Press Family, for being pillars of strength as I build fictional worlds with my words.

There is no better way to make things happen than to grab every opportunity and create our own steps to success. God will always guide us towards greatness.

ABOUT THE AUTHOR

Monica Sahu is a Banker turned Writer. After her Bachelor's Degree in Hotel and Hospitality Administration and her time in the World of Finance, she found her artistic passion in content creation. Her social media presence mainly focuses on Body Positivity, Fitness, Sustainability, Realism, Ethical Marketing and Tech Trends. She has been featured by multiple media platforms including major national and international print media, for advocating Body Positive Fitness and Breaking Body Stereotypes. In her free time, she enjoys listening to music, traveling and exploring different forms of artistic expression.

You can find her on Instagram, X (formerly known as Twitter) and Facebook. Direct Links to her major social media platforms are attached to her Notion Press profile. Her drabbles and short stories are also available online.

You can tag her and Notion Press on your creative pictures and reviews of this book or DM her the same. She is always eager to connect with new talents, support artists and engage with her readers, audiences and digital family.

CONNECT WITH US

Follow us for latest updates on new book releases, events & book festivals, digital contests, giveaways and much more.

Creative contents featuring this series, including pictures of the books, vlogs, spoiler-free reviews, fan artwork, purchase order screenshot, blog features, etc. will be shared on the Author's social media platforms. So, make sure to follow and tag us.

	Monica Sahu	Notion Press
Facebook	www.facebook.com /monica.sahu	www.facebook.com /notionpress
Instagram	@monica25101990	@notion.press
X	@monica25101990 @monicas2510	@notionpress

ENJOY THE SERIES

A FAMILY OF STRANGERS

(Thriller • Drama • Dark Romance)

THE STRANGE REALITY

(Psychological Horror • Twisted • Thriller)

KISS ME WITH YOUR DOE EYES

(Thriller • Romance • Humor • Healing)